a fine mess

alison stone

A FINE MESS is available in ebook and print:

Ebook ISBN: 978-1-964598-05-5

Print ISBN: 978-1-964598-06-2

elizabeth

I turned my back to brace against the howling wind whipping off Lake Erie and sipped my Timmy Ho's double-double coffee and scanned the landscape. It wasn't exactly a brilliant decision to stroll along the inner harbor to capture a photo of Buffalo City Hall against a backdrop of silver clouds, but at least the biting wind gave me something to feel other than sorry for myself.

I tugged off one mitten with my teeth and adjusted my hat down over my ears. I yanked up the zipper on my coat, rated for thirty-five degrees below zero (I had, after all, recently moved back from Boston), and tucked my chin into the collar. My ex used to say, "There's no bad weather, just bad clothing." Turned out he lied. About a lot of things.

Including his cute little side chick.

Dismissing the thought, I set down the paper coffee cup on the parking curb, tucked one mitten under my arm, and lifted the camera from the strap around my neck. It was one of those expensive ones that had a lens cap and an instruction booklet, not an app on my iPhone.

Click. Click. Click.

Another breeze kicked up and sent the coffee cup skittering across the parking lot like a cockroach exposed to sudden daylight. Groaning, I took off in pursuit, my camera on its strap thumping heavily against my chest. Thankfully, the wind died down long enough for me to stomp on the cup, crushing it. I didn't want anyone calling me a litterbug. After properly disposing of the trash, I checked the image on the camera's screen.

Not bad.

I'd take a few more just in case, then pick the best one. A pithy caption would come to me on the drive home, and then I'd post it on social media.

And wait for likes and comments.

This was what my world had boiled down to.

My friends, most of whom I had gone to school with while in Boston, thought it was bizarre that I chose to move to Buffalo after getting laid off from a top architectural firm in Beantown. Apparently they had bought into the bad press that Buffalo was boring, blue-collar, and bitterly cold. Like Boston couldn't be wicked cold, too? What they failed to consider was that the second-largest city in New York State had a rich tradition of gorgeous architecture by the likes of Frank Lloyd Wright. But that wasn't the primary reason I had moved (back) to the Queen City. Buffalo was home, or more accurately, the closest city to Walleye Point, a small town on Lake Erie where I'd lived between the ages of twelve and eighteen. As a wide-eyed college freshman, I had told my Boston roommates I was from New York, but to them, that automatically meant New York City. If I corrected them to say that, no, not New York City, but rather Walleye Point, it was inevitably followed by a geography lesson. My hometown was forty-five minutes outside of Buffalo. If they weren't staring at me like an open-mouthed dead fish, they were laughing at the name. So, my simple answer when asked where I was from became Buffalo. People knew Buffalo, even if the conversation inevitably turned to snow, chicken wings, and the Bills' *really* good—or *really* bad—season, depending on the year.

So here I was, back in the Queen City after getting laid off. It had coincided with the end of my expensive lease in Boston, so it made sense. Housing was more affordable here. I'd floated my résumé out to local firms, and while I waited, I'd finally get around to starting that Instagram account documenting the architecture in and around Buffalo. Perhaps if I grew my online presence, I could open my own design firm. Not my exact field of study, but wealthy people loved to spend money on all sorts of stuff for their homes. I'd get to flip through magazines and pick out fancy lamps and cutting-edge furniture like the chill designers I envied in my old office. (A bunch of them had been let go, too, but I was confident they hadn't moved to Buffalo to find employment.) I wouldn't have to use my hard-earned degree, but I also wouldn't have to double- and triple-check my math to make sure a new high-rise building wouldn't come tumbling down under the weight of all those Amazon deliveries.

Releasing a long breath, I turned my attention to the downtown skyline. The silvery storm clouds parted, and a ray of sunshine broke through. I snapped a few more shots, framing them with the silvery clouds and bare branches of a nearby tree. I loved this aesthetic.

A dark shadow at my feet made me jump to the side, then I laughed at myself when the little dog followed me, sniffing at my sneakers. "Well, hello there." I bent down and tickled the cute pup under his chin. "Are you lost?" Out of the corner of my eye, I saw a young woman jogging our way.

"Sorry about that. He's friendly," the woman called out, waving the leash in her hand while jogging in place. "There's usually no one else in the harbor when it's this cold."

I wondered if she'd ever heard a dog owner bold enough to claim their off-leash dog (against the law per the posted signs, by the way) was a terror and likely to take your fingers off if you weren't careful. But I wasn't in the mood for confrontation and besides, I was a huge dog person.

"What's his name?" I asked.

"Paul."

"Paul?" I laughed.

The woman might have blushed, or her cheeks were merely flush from the cold. "He came with that name when I adopted him."

"Hello, Paul." The little black dog stopped sniffing and looked up. "I see you know your name."

"Exactly. That's why I couldn't change it." The woman hooked the leash to his collar. "I work from home, and I need to tire him out; otherwise he barks like a fool when I'm on a Zoom call." The woman went back to jogging in place and rubbed her hands together. "I can't wait until it gets warmer."

"Me, too." It was already mid-April, but the weather felt more like February. Patches of dirty snow remained, which the locals fondly called "snirt."

My phone rang in my pocket and I instinctively put my hand over it to silence it.

Paul's owner lifted her purple mitten and waved. "Stay warm."

"You, too." I turned to face the downtown skyline over the boat harbor. Little exchanges like the one with the jogger had been the extent of my social interactions since moving here. Fine by me. I wasn't the chatty type. I preferred behind-the-scenes—or the phone screen—which made my new business idea seem like a perfect fit.

I needed to make it work. My severance would only last six months. I'd have to act fast and be frugal.

My belly grumbled. Did being thrifty mean I couldn't grab a burrito from my favorite takeout place? Surely a yummy lunch wouldn't put me in the red. Yet.

I hustled across the empty parking lot and climbed into the rental, hoping I could find permanent living accommodations near public transportation. For now, I had to pony up for a weekly rental room in one of those converted motels rendered obsolete when expressways diverted travelers from Main Street.

This time when my phone dinged, I fished it out of my pocket. An unfamiliar number was displayed on the screen. "Figures," I muttered to myself. "Spammy call." I tossed the phone on the passenger seat and started the car. I was about to pull away when the voicemail alert drew my attention, making my heart drop. Voicemails usually meant something important. A job? Maybe I had been too quick to ignore the call.

Hurriedly, I tapped the buttons with fat thumbs and put the message on speaker. "Hello, Lizzy"—no one has called me that since high school— "this is Cassie Parker." Now it makes sense. Warm tingles spread across my skin at the name. "I'm not sure if you remember me." *Yeah, I remember.* "We went to Walleye Middle and High together. Anyway… I'm rambling…" I listened intently, bringing to mind twelve-year-old Cassie Parker. One of my first friends when I moved to Walleye Point. Nothing like the dull ache of a long-ago betrayal to sour my mood.

"I'm a nurse practitioner at Walleye Community Hospital. Your grandmother has been admitted. I got this number from her emergency contact list on her phone. Um, can you call me back? It's urgent." Cassie rattled off both the number for the hospital and her personal cell.

With my heart beating in my throat, I dialed the woman's cell, bracing for the worst. When was the last time I spoke to Lin? A few weeks ago? I purposely haven't called because I didn't want to tell her I had been laid off. My grandmother wasn't exactly the comforting type. I learned that the hard way after my mother died when I was left to navigate the perils of my teenage years living with a grandmother who resented me in a small town of mean girls.

Or maybe girls were just mean at that age. Period.

It came as no surprise that I had been home only once in the past ten years. I had made offers of plane tickets and fun weekends in Boston that Lin—a nickname that I bestowed on my grandmother when I was a toddler and had unsuccessfully tried to sound out Linda—refused. We both knew Lin wouldn't travel, but it was a game we played. We wanted to create the illusion we had a relationship without the effort of sustaining one.

Despite all that, I was grateful Lin spared me from foster care after Mom died. Lin had struggled to raise a daughter and was less than thrilled to have to do it again when it came to me.

A mixture of nostalgia, resentment and worry settled in my belly when I replayed the message from my so-called childhood friend. *Lin is in the hospital.* Was I going to be one of those people in that Scotty McCreery song, wishing I had five more minutes?

elizabeth

Believe it or not, I had to use Google Maps to find the hospital in my own hometown. Despite Lin's bitterness at acquiring a kid late in life, she had apparently taken good care of me because I have no memories of ever being there, not that I would remember how to get there.

The entire drive to Walleye Point had been a complete blur after learning my grandmother had suffered a stroke and was unconscious. I was eager for more information, but Cassie, the nurse practitioner in the ICU, didn't have any.

I slammed on the brakes and glanced in the rearview mirror, relieved that no one was tailgating me. That's all I needed. I had almost missed the small hospital sign behind the branches of a cherry blossom tree whose buds had been confused by last week's seventy-degree temperatures. The foggy windshield and the inclement weather made visibility worse.

I pulled into a visitor's spot and slowly uncurled my fingers from their death grip on the steering wheel. I stared at the small-town hospital, rationalizing that if Lin was in really bad shape, they wouldn't have told me to come here, right? Lin would have been sent to one of the major hospitals in

Buffalo, or Erie, Pennsylvania. Those hospitals specialized in treating stroke victims, touting their recovery rates.

Oh shoot, oh shoot, oh shoot. A flush of tingles raced across my scalp and up my arms. *What if I'm too late?* What if the ambulance rushed Lin here because it wasn't worth a trip to a larger town? Specialty hospitals could save lives. *Any* hospital could declare someone dead.

Stop, stop, stop. Sitting here and imagining the worst wasn't doing me any favors. I steeled myself and got out of the car and strode toward the hospital, oblivious to the wind whipping my hair. The automatic doors whooshed open before I had a chance to tap the square handicap button. Like a good rule follower, I stopped at security, produced ID, then reluctantly slapped on a sticker with an image of my driver's license. I glanced down and frowned. The goofy photo shot at a harshly lit DMV was the least of my problems right now.

My pulse thrummed in my ears as I followed the signs up to the ICU. A second set of doors swung open. The sterility of the intensive care unit, with its glass-walled rooms and machines, sent another memory tickling the recesses of my mind. I folded my arms tightly across my chest, wrinkling the badge in the folds of my coat.

At least no one could see my awful license photo anymore.

I slowed at the nurses' station. Dots danced in the periphery of my vision, and I felt a little woozy. I unzipped my coat and released a breath between narrowed lips.

"May I help you?" a nurse asked.

"I'm looking…" My words trailed off as the name on a white placard next to the doorframe came into focus: *Linda Graham.*

My soul left my body as I drifted closer. My feisty grandmother—Lin—lay chillingly still, an oxygen tube draped under her nostrils. Machines monitored her vitals. Her huge presence had been reduced to this tiny, frail woman under a white blanket in this sterile space.

Unable to peel my eyes away, I pressed my hand to my chest and whispered, "...for my grandmother." But I found her.

Snapping out of my trance, I glanced around, realizing the nurse hadn't followed me. I rushed to my grandmother's bedside and folded Lin's cold and lifeless hand into mine.

"You'd do anything to get me to come home, wouldn't you?" My voice cracked with emotion. If I let the tears fall, they'd never stop. Hot blood chugged through my veins and the glass walls pulsed. I found a chair and dragged it next to the bed. I collapsed and rested my forehead on the older woman's hand.

"Lizzy?"

A familiar voice pulled me out of prayer, if you could call pleading *Please God don't let her die* over and over a prayer.

Wearing a purple hoodie over stylish scrubs in the same shade, Cassie Parker stood at the foot of the bed. "You made it." Her eyes flashed recognition as we both seemed to take in the adult version of the teens we had once known. I would have recognized Cassie even without the ID hanging around her neck on a WPCH lanyard. I squinted to read the logo: *Reeling in Wellness at Walleye Point Community Hospital.* I wondered how much they paid some marketing genius for that one.

I lifted my gaze to find Cassie looking at me with a puzzled expression. I cleared my throat. "Yeah, I got on the road immediately after we talked." I stood and pressed a kiss to the crown of my grandmother's head. The familiar smell of her shampoo tickled my nose, making me feel both nostalgic and remorseful. *Why did I stay away?* "I'll be right back, Lin." I gestured toward Cassie, urging her to follow me outside the glass-enclosed space. "Has there been any change?" I whispered.

"No."

"Who found her?" Lin was a young sixty-four. She was too young to have a stroke. *Wishful thinking?*

"She was at the grocery store when she had trouble walking, and she started slurring her speech. Thankfully the cashier recognized she was having some sort of medical event. Your grandmother lost consciousness before the ambulance arrived."

Cassie's words sounded like they were coming through a very long tunnel. I flattened my cool palm against my fiery cheek. How likely was it that I was going to pass out right now?

Focus. I blinked rapidly, trying to still the room swaying around me.

"They'll want to run more tests to confirm if it truly was a stroke." Perhaps recognizing the clear panic on my face, Cassie reached out and touched my arm. "She's getting the best care. And it was a good thing that she was at the grocery store when it happened. If she had been at home—"

"Is she in a coma?" I interrupted and glanced at Lin, her jaw slack and her mouth gaping open. It physically pained me to think of Lin alone in her little bungalow, her pleas for help going unanswered.

"Her brain needs time to heal." A polite non-answer.

"Will she be okay?" I considered myself a smart woman— I knew there were no guarantees. But I wanted one, *really* wanted one. A darn promise that my grandma was going to be okay.

"The extent of her recovery is yet to be seen. The doctor will provide more information when she comes in," Cassie responded, clearly having a lot of practice dealing with distraught family members.

A lump formed in my throat, and I suddenly felt like throwing up.

Cassie must have sensed my distress and rushed to my side. "Are you okay? I'll get you water."

Rendered mute, I nodded. The edges of my vision grew fuzzy, and I didn't want to take an ounce of attention away from the care of my grandmother or the other patients in the ICU. But, OMG, I could not spew what little I had in my stomach on the worn tile floor.

Breathe in. Breathe out.

Cassie disappeared for a second and returned with a plastic cup of water. I took a few sips, and the world began to right itself. "Thank you."

"No worries." Cassie smiled tightly. "I'm surprised you were able to get here so quickly. I heard you stayed in Boston after college." She lifted an eyebrow in expectation.

I nodded, amazed that anyone in Walleye had noticed my absence. *It is a small town.* "I was in Buffalo when you called."

"Ah, that makes sense," Cassie said, seeming to calculate the driving time between Walleye Point and Buffalo versus here and Boston. "Oh, so Buffalo's home?"

"Yeah." If a cheap week-to-week rental qualified. The fewer details I fed the rumor mill, the better. Yet I had no idea why I'd be of interest to anyone now.

"Well, if you need anything…" The woman who had been a classic mean girl in middle school had apparently changed her ways. Or, more than likely, being pleasant to patients and their families was part of the job.

Whether or not Cassie Parker deserved my cynicism didn't matter. I wasn't myself. Not with Lin here in the ICU. "I'm fine. Don't let me hold you up. You must be busy." I wanted her to leave because I was afraid I was going to snap at her.

"My shift is over. I just wanted to make sure your grandmother has everything she needs before I left."

"That was nice of you." Really nice. A fraction of my

disdain for the woman drained from my hardened heart. Maybe people did change.

Cassie laughed quietly. "Surprised?" She hesitated a fraction. "I'm not the same person I was when we were twelve. I always—" She shook her head and seemed to swallow the words, as if now wasn't the time to bring up the past.

"None of us are the same." I waved my hand in a dismissive gesture, not wanting to acknowledge that my humiliation at the hands of Cassie and friends at a birthday slumber party was a core memory that shaped my childhood in Walleye Point. Shaped my distrust of people's true intentions.

Reliving the past held no appeal.

Especially right now.

"Look at you." Cassie gestured with a wave of her hand at my designer coat and handbag, impulsive purchases meant to help me fit in with my fellow Boston commuters, people who likely had better-paying jobs than I had. Only other entry-level architects seemed to know how poorly paid we were.

"Look at *you*," I mimicked, quickly deflecting the attention away from myself. I was well dressed—*even if I say so myself*—but I still hated drawing attention to myself. It was too reminiscent of kids pointing out my Goodwill clothes back in high school. "I see you returned to your natural brown hair."

Cassie dragged a loose strand through her fingers. "Keeping up the blonde was more effort than it was worth."

I shrugged, eager to shift the focus back to Lin. "Thank you for calling me. And taking the time to update me." A piece of grit under a contact lens sent my left eye into a spasm. I wanted to pop it out, but I hadn't grabbed my glasses in my rush to leave Buffalo.

"Can I get you anything, Lizzy?"

The sound of my childhood nickname scraped across my already frayed nerves. I forced a laugh. "No one has called me that since high school. I go by Elizabeth now."

"Oh, sure." Cassie's cheeks fired red, as if she had been

scolded, and I immediately felt bad for correcting the woman. Adult Cassie, by all accounts, seemed like a decent person.

I drew in a deep breath. "Lin's condition is a matter of wait and see?" I had never done well with the unpredictable.

"This type of acute episode takes its own time to heal. Dr. Smythe, the neurosurgeon, will give you a full update." Cassie checked her watch. "Probably tomorrow." She fastened the bottom of the zipper on her hoodie and slid it up to mid-chest. "I'm off the next two days, but feel free to call if you have any questions. You can also reach the nurses' station. And, of course, you're welcome to stay for as long as you'd like." Cassie lowered her voice. "Visiting hours run from ten a.m. to eight p.m."

My gaze drifted to the clock on the wall. It was just after three in the afternoon. "Thank you."

Cassie touched my arm. "Talk to her. Let her know you're here."

"Okay." I pressed a finger to my temple. A headache pulsed behind my eyes. I blinked, and the room went blurry. Unease sloshed in my gut at the thought of driving back to Buffalo with wonky vision.

"Please don't hesitate to call. I mean it," Cassie said, taking a step backward toward the door.

"I will." I smiled tightly, sensing a thread of tension between us despite our pleasantries. Or maybe I was projecting. No matter how much time had passed, I still had a visceral reaction when reminded of certain childhood events.

Cassie hesitated a beat, then said, "It's nice to see you. It really is." She lingered for a moment. "It's tough to come home under these circumstances."

I was about to rub my eye but stopped short, afraid I'd lose the contact lens altogether. "Coming back to Walleye Point is hard no matter what the circumstances." Had I just opened mouth, inserted foot? After all, Cassie had never left.

Yet I had never wanted to return.

3 /
nicholas

I wasn't usually at the office this early in the morning, but I couldn't sleep. I decided to stop in and check the real estate listings. Turned out Mrs. Ralston had the same idea. Although honestly, it didn't matter. She would have gotten hold of me either way.

Stupid cell phones. If my livelihood didn't depend on being accessible, I'd toss mine in the lake.

Holding the phone out in front of me on speaker, I settled into the leather ergonomic chair and tried to stay focused on the conversation and not the hard lumbar support jamming into my lower back.

"The house won't be on the market for long," Barbara Ralston said. "Did you line up an appointment for me and Dale to see it?"

I had sent an email last night—Dale's requested form of communication—letting the couple know that the owners of that property would not conduct any showings until the weekend. But of course, she and her husband weren't communicating, an issue that now became my problem.

"Are you listening?" Mrs. Ralston snapped at me over the phone, much like my teachers had done when I was daydreaming. "I was told Moretti Realty was the best on the Point." I rolled my eyes at her passive-aggressive dig.

The people who lived here only during the summer called it *the Point*. Everyone else referred to the small town as Walleye or Walleye Point, its official name. Like normal people.

"I *must* have a lake view. Absolutely must," she continued. I plucked a ballpoint pen out of the mug on the desk and doodled on a pad of paper.

"Of course." *Doesn't everyone?* "We'll get you in to see this property first thing. On Saturday." I lowered the phone, hoping Mrs. Ralston didn't hear my frustrated sigh. She was a client after all. I spun the chair to face the window. The view from the second-floor office always cheered me up. Most of the boat slips in the harbor were empty, but that would change once the weather broke. This place came to life during the summer, a season too short to appease my former girlfriend who decided to question all her life choices—including me—after one December lake-effect snowstorm.

One. I had lived through a lifetime of winds whipping off the water. Bands dumping feet of snow on my small hometown. The real possibility of a day off from school had me and all my hockey buddies wearing our PJs inside out and flushing ice cubes down the toilet. We were all a superstitious bunch.

A fresh breeze wafted through the screen. Ah, the promise of spring. In a few hours, the scent of fried seafood and my grandmother's sauce would seep through the floorboards from the restaurant below. Moretti Realty and Construction could easily afford a less aromatic office, but views like this were rare. Hence the frantic client on the other end of the phone eager to claim her own lake view.

"Does ten o'clock work for you?" I asked after giving her a reasonable amount of time to vent.

"Oh." She sounded deflated. "Do we really have to wait

until Saturday?" Her sweet-as-honey tone suggested she was a woman used to getting her way. "I'm sure you can pull a few strings."

The request seemed more like a challenge; one I couldn't bother to accept. The homeowners were in the cat's seat with a newer build on a small patch of lakefront land. Move-in ready with beach access, without a lot of property to maintain. "Let's plan on Saturday at ten. I'll call if something changes." My thumb hovered over the end button.

"You do that." Mrs. Ralston's words came out clipped.

I spun to face the desk, realizing I might regret sounding dismissive. "I can see if there are any other properties available."

Mrs. Ralston let out a noise of derision. *As if.*

Ignoring her obvious skepticism, I wiggled the mouse, and the computer screen came to life. I clicked through the listings. Nowadays, most people haunted the real estate websites on their mobile phones while having coffee and scones at the local cafe, distractedly listening to their children/partners/friends and only reaching out to me once they located what they hoped would be their dream home. But Mrs. Ralston was either technologically challenged or had no interest in doing her own research. Maybe both.

I had come to understand why my father, Joseph Moretti Jr.—Junior for short—was turning over most of the operation of his company to his three sons. It had been started by my grandfather with a restaurant, the one downstairs, then expanded to real estate and then construction. Personally, I wouldn't be sorry to see the real estate arm go. If that was my father's plan.

I read the listings, knowing by heart which addresses had the views my clients demanded. I forced a smile, hoping it might translate over the call even though I felt like clawing my eyes out. "Are you willing to consider fixer-uppers?" Most people looking for a summer cottage didn't want something that required work. They wanted a turnkey so they could drive down from Buffalo, stare at the lake for the weekend, then go home for their Monday-through-Friday jobs.

Lather. Rinse. Repeat.

Vacation.

Unless, of course, they had money. Lots of it. Then all bets were off. These clients didn't care about construction overruns, eager to bring some of the old homes back to life. Homes of former Buffalo millionaires made wealthy at the turn of the twentieth century. And it was these rich conservationists that kept the construction arm of the Moretti business flush. That was more my jam. I had studied civil engineering in college but never graduated.

It was Mrs. Ralston's turn to sigh. "I've been looking at some homes on Crystal Beach, but I'd prefer not to go across the border."

When Covid shut the US-Canada border for an extended period, the summer homeowners who couldn't access their cottages had come to rethink the location of their second—or third—homes along Lake Erie. The summers in this part of the world were gorgeous, but short. Missing even a few had been devastating, making many lake-home shoppers hesitant to invest north of the border. All good news for my family's business here in Western New York.

"I understand completely. I do, however, have two smaller cottages that have great views on the Point." I cringed. *The Point.* "Both need work."

"Well, okay," she said, seeming to consider. "When can you show them to me?"

"I'm sure I could line up all appointments for Saturday. This way you don't have to make multiple trips."

"That would be wonderful," she said, sounding genuinely pleased.

As much as I disliked aspects of my job, I was good at them. No one would ever say the charming Nicholas Moretti didn't have a way with people. I forced another smile. "I'll email you and Dale with the addresses and times."

"Fantastic."

I made a note on a Post-it to join the growing pile on my desk. I'd enter them in my phone later.

As I was wrapping up the call, my brother Dominic appeared in the doorway with his tanned arms crossed over his bulky chest. Dom never missed a workout or a chance to get more sun. He had been in the Florida Keys for most of April and wasn't supposed to return until May first. I tossed my phone on the desk and leaned back. What was up with the lumbar support?

"Holding down the fort?" Dominic asked. "Showing homes to bored empty nesters?"

"Got it under control," I said dryly, careful not to let my brother see how much I hated this job sometimes. Dom would glom onto my bad mood and ratchet up his barbs to try to get his half-brother going. I no longer showed my rage —I had learned to control my emotions as a teen—but man, my brother loved to try. "Thought you weren't coming home for a couple more weeks," I said, affecting a bored tone.

"Di has a follow-up doctor's appointment." His wife had a cancer scare last summer. He ran his hand across his full head of dark hair and lowered his gaze, a rare show of empathy and concern by my self-involved brother. "We have a flight to Florida tomorrow night. I have a golf tournament this weekend."

There's the guy I know so well.

"With Sal?" The eldest Moretti brother.

"Who else? We've got a friendly wager on the game." Dom adjusted his stance, as he was preparing to guard the goal in a soccer match—the one other sport we all squeezed in around hockey. "He's such a sucker."

The three Moretti brothers were always in a tight competition—for everything. But most of the dreck flowed downhill from oldest to youngest, in my direction. I suspected it was because they never forgave my mom for being the other woman and wrecking their home. And when I came along, there was a third son to share Junior's vast wealth.

As if I had any control over any of that.

Dom gestured with his chin toward the computer monitor. "Got any good listings?"

"Mostly fixer-uppers."

"I hate being a tour guide for the lookie-loos who have more time than money." Dom seemed as bored as he sounded.

"Mr. Ralston plays tennis with Dad. They have money." I gritted my teeth, hating the compulsion to justify myself.

Dom twirled his index finger in the air. "Whoopie."

I entered Saturday's appointment into my phone calendar to pass the time, then looked up at my hovering brother. "What's up?"

Dom dragged a chair over, spun it around, then straddled it and rested his beefy arms across the top rail. Meatball had been his nickname in high school. Few dared to call him that to his face. But secretly it was gratifying for me as a kid because I sensed a kinship with the guys who mocked my brother behind his back. Dom really could be a jerk.

Dom steepled his hands, tapping the pads of his fingers. "You know the Langmore property that Dad had his eye on for years…"

I furrowed my brow. "Yeah, is it up for sale?" I reached for the mouse and shook it. How had I missed that?

Dominic's lips spread into a wide grin. "Oh, little brother, we don't wait for listings to pop up on the MLS like the common folk. We get out in front of them."

"Do tell, then," I said dryly.

"My sources tell me Mrs. Langmore moved into hospice last month." He checked his phone, then lowered it. "She can't have long."

"Kinda heartless." Even for Dom. If that was what it took to snag the best listings, count me out.

"It's business." Dom leaned forward and thumped his fingers on the front of the desk, then stood and swung the chair back around and pushed it against the wall in what appeared to be a practiced move. "Old Lady Langmore has to be a hundred years old, easy."

I sniffed. "I'll keep my eye out for the listing."

Dominic scoffed. "Keep your eye out? No, you have to be proactive. Come on, let's go check it out."

"You check it out." I felt a little icky about swooping in before the poor woman was even six feet under. I gestured to the phone's blinking voicemail indicator, not sure when I had missed that call. Perhaps when I was talking to Mrs. Ralston on my cell. Junior had been reluctant to give up the landline. "I'll man the phone line while you're gone." The lameness of my excuse rang in my ears. It was worth a shot.

"Redirect the calls to your cell and come on."

I reclined in my chair and stuffed my hand behind my lower back. This chair was the worst.

"Come on," Dom repeated. "You need to step up since I'm headed back out of town. Show Dad you have what it takes."

A muscle ticked in my jaw. *I will not take the bait. I will not take the bait.*

"It would kill Sal if someone other than him landed this deal. You got to do this for both of us."

If the three Moretti brothers weren't duking it out against one another, a pair of us was teaming up against the odd man out. Apparently today it was Sal. We had been groomed since birth to take over Moretti Realty and Construction, but there was a hierarchy. The eldest, Sal, being at the top.

Dom jerked his head toward the door. "Let's go." He gestured to the iPad resting on the corner of the desk. "Grab it. We can do a quick survey of the land while we're there. Come up with an offer."

"And bother Mrs. Langmore in hospice?" My tone made no mistake that I wasn't going to be negotiating a lowball deal while the woman was dying. I might be looking to climb to the top but not over bodies.

"Maybe she has family hanging around looking to unload the property. We'll be doing them a favor."

"You mean family who are about to lose their loved one?" I slowly shook my head. How was it possible that I am related to this merciless lunkhead?

"Our offer will ease their pain." Dom's somber tone was undermined by the gleeful look in his eyes. He patted the doorframe with his open palm. "Let's *goooo*." He slowed at the door, checked his cell phone, and immediately began tapping away. "It's hard to find comps on the Langmore property. That will work in our favor. Lowball them. I'm sure the house needs repairs. We'll use that to our advantage. Besides, the whole thing is going to be razed."

"So much for easing the grieving family's pain," Nicholas deadpanned as he stood and came around the desk.

Dom playfully punched my arm. "We're businessmen, not a charity."

I scrubbed a hand across my whiskers, another thing to annoy me. I really should have shaved this morning. "I'll check out the property with you because it's my job, not because you're telling me to."

"Whatever gets you there."

4 /
elizabeth

The first thing I did when I woke up bright and early the next morning in my cramped, dated rental in Buffalo was to call the hospital in Walleye Point. Satisfied that my grandmother was stable, I packed a bag, including my prescription glasses this time, and drove straight to the little bungalow on the shore of Lake Erie. While there, I'd grab a few personal items that might make Lin's hospital stay more comfortable. Hopefully a key was still under a potted plant on the front porch. If not, perhaps Mrs. Langmore who owned the main house on the property could let me in.

A smile curved my lips at the thought of the kindly lady who employed my grandmother. Gosh, she must be really old by now. Another pang of guilt reminded me that I had allowed too much time to pass between visits.

The early morning traffic on the westbound Thruway was light, and I reached the Langmore residence in less than an hour. Lin lived in a bungalow located beyond the main house, closer to the lake. I turned on the directional but stopped when I noticed a chain stretched across the stone driveway with a *No Trespassing* sign hanging askew. The place reeked of abandonment, but how could that be? Lin had only been admitted to the hospital yesterday. And my grandmother took great pride in managing the property. A strange blend of grief and nostalgia pressed in on my lungs, making it hard to take a deep breath.

It was this place. This town.

Frowning, I parked at the curb and hopped out. The soft breeze from the lake on my face eased the knot between my shoulder blades. What an unexpected treat for early April. I rolled my shoulders and filled my lungs with a cleansing breath.

Please, Grandma, be okay. I promise I'll come visit more often.

Why had I stayed away for so long?

I knew why. It was easier to forget my past when I didn't have to face daily reminders.

You're not that same person you were back then.

Focus. Focus. Focus.

Go check on Lin's place, then check on her.

I had developed a habit of creating mental to-do lists when I got overwhelmed. I had grown up surrounded by chaos. Turning to structure and order had gotten me far in life. It calmed the panic.

It got me through college.

It would get me through everything that was going on now, too.

I glanced up at Mrs. Langmore's Victorian house and found myself smiling again. The once white siding had grown dingy gray and chipped. There was a slight part in the curtains on the second story, and I waved. Because of the reflection on the glass, I had no way of knowing if Mrs. Langmore was inside watching me. I didn't want to be rude. My gaze drifted upward and a powerful wave of nostalgia made the back of my eyes tingle. When I first moved here, I dreamed about what it would be like to have an art studio in the room at the very top. My grandmother had explained that the outdoor space surrounding my dream studio was a widow's walk. This conjured up romantic images of a young bride in a gown flapping in the wind, waiting for her husband to return from an expedition to some far-flung corner of the Great Lakes or beyond.

Even as a child, I had understood grief.

Or maybe I had spent too much of my lonely childhood reading gothic novels with fantastic atmospheric estates. My escape.

Once Mrs. Langmore had allowed me to step out onto the weatherworn planks, affording me a panoramic view of Lake Erie surrounded by the tangy sweet smell of algae. Young me had scanned the vast body of water, imagining all the potential that lay beyond tiny Walleye.

I held onto that vision—the wind whipping my hair, the tingles in my belly as I began to realize there was more. More than here in Walleye Point. *So much more.* It was this knowledge that spurred me on to do well in school, to get into a top college, to leave this small town that had destroyed my mother and anchored Lin to the only place she had ever known.

Besides giving fuel to my wanderlust, that brief trip onto the observation platform had been the moment my interest in architecture had taken root. Some creative visionary had designed that feature.

I could do that.

Strong emotions clogged my throat as I let my gaze caress each and every detail of the old Victorian like an old friend. Things I had long ago memorized, just as I had studied the features of the Temple of Concordia in Greece and the Byzantine churches while in school. A vine of dead leaves traveled up and wound its way around the circular window above the main entryway. This place wasn't as well-kept as it used to be.

I slid my "boyfriend bag"—a birthday gift from my college roommate—off my shoulder and set it on the grass.

Strange, I had yet to use it to spend the night at a boyfriend's house, a point that was lost neither on me nor my friend.

"You can't be too prepared," Malissa had said, then laughed, something that might have sounded condescending if it had come from anyone but her, the one person I could always rely on.

I grabbed my cell phone from the side pocket and tapped on the camera app. This would have to do since I didn't have my expensive camera with me. I turned in a slow circle. The rope swing still hung from a solid branch of the maple tree in the front yard. Its seat had been old even when I was a child, but despite the threat of a splinter, I'd jump on the wooden seat and pump my legs. Once I got going, I'd stretch my toes to the sky, a sock poking out through worn sneakers. I wouldn't dare trust the discolored and frayed rope now. It seemed time had tried to reclaim the land, the house. The flagstone pathway and gardens Mrs. Langmore had lovingly tended were overgrown. My grandmother was thirty-plus years younger than her employer, yet it appeared she hadn't been able to maintain the property either.

The ghosts from my past gathered around me now that I was back here. I had been so eager to leave Walleye Point that I had forgot to savor the sweet, everyday moments of living in this magical place. Was that hollowness in my chest longing?

Shaking off the heavy feelings, I aimed my phone camera at the weathervane at the peak of Mrs. Langmore's house. Mentally, I composed possible hashtags for a social media post:

#Victorian
#LakeErieWidowsWalk
#HomeSweetHome

An idea started to formulate. There was no need to limit my online content to Buffalo—I could take photos of architecture and beauty that could be found, and potentially overlooked, anywhere. Maybe center on a lake theme. My former boss had told me I had a good eye.

Some good that did me when it was time for layoffs.

Baby steps. I'd build my portfolio. Create posts. Eventually do livestreams even though the idea made my skin crawl. I preferred working behind the scenes. But it might be worth it if I could get the views, attract sponsors, and make money from my content…and stay in Walleye Point while my grandmother recovered. The realization that I'd have to nurse Lin back to health flopped like a cold wet rag on the new spark of my ideas. The older woman would likely be a difficult patient.

One thing at a time.

I snapped a series of photos from various angles. A tinge of excitement tickled the back of my neck as the creativity I had thought died with my termination notice sparked to life. I scrolled through the images, then at the surrounding Langmore property. I couldn't put off the inevitable any longer. I'd have to pick up a few things from Lin's home then zip up to the hospital.

What if Lin never recovers?

My intrusive thoughts had a way of nagging me at the most inappropriate times. I refused to allow them to render me immobile, creating a mental list: *Grab Grandma's toothbrush, robe, and her favorite throw from the couch. You can handle that. Simple. Keep it simple.*

I drummed my fingers on the side of my leg, my nervous energy seeking an outlet. The sound of gravel crunching underfoot made me snap my head around, and I sucked in a breath. Two broad figures, their features shadowed by the dappled light filtering through the mature trees, were strolling up the driveway. My fight-or-flight response kicked in and I debated ducking behind a tree, then laughed to myself at the ridiculousness of it. Nope! Not now. I had done the same thing when I was the new kid in town, trying to hide from the approaching bus because I hated, *hated* school. The one time I had been successful at dodging the morning bus, my grandmother stormed out of the house, grabbed me by the arm, shoved me into the car, muttering how I had been a dang-fool and all this idiocy had only served to make Lin late for work. Mrs. Langmore had expected her to do her job without any drama.

Fat chance when it came to a lonely orphan and a frustrated grandmother.

There was never any discussion as to why I had such a strong dislike for school. It didn't matter. Lin was practical to a fault. She didn't believe in discussing things ad nauseam. Why labor over something that wasn't going to change? I had to go to school. Period.

Once again, forced to face something I couldn't avoid, I crossed my arms and waited for the pair to approach. I scanned the street beyond the wrought-iron fence of the vast estate. Surely someone would hear me if I screamed. *Stop obsessing.* The demeanor and dress of the men struck me as more Walleye Point summer people than drifters looking to hit me up for some cash. Or worse.

A whisper of dread made the flesh on my arms prickle. I had been wrong before.

One had a baseball cap pulled low and seemed to be taking in the old house, much as I had done. The other was engrossed in his cell phone. Neither struck me as hunters stalking their prey. Gosh, I really needed to cut back on the dark-themed novels I devoured during my long, lonely nights.

"Can I help you?" I purposely clipped each word, trying to sound peeved that someone had the nerve to wander onto the property. Acting like it was mine. If I was lucky, they'd apologize and leave. However, maybe Mrs. Langmore was expecting them and then I'd look like a "Karen" who stuck my nose where it didn't belong. My cheeks grew hot at the notion of embarrassing myself.

"Oh, hello," Baseball Cap Guy said, as if he hadn't expected anyone to be here. I supposed it was a logical conclusion, but it didn't explain why he was here.

"Can I help you?" I repeated, forcing a smile to soften the edge of my pointed question. If they were solicitors, I didn't want them to think I was a pushover. However, even though these men were dressed casually, the brands and fit screamed money. They were not trying to sell me anything, except maybe a line of bull.

I couldn't exactly pinpoint why I felt this way.

The first man lowered his phone, seemingly unconcerned by my presence. *That's annoying.* "I tracked down Mrs. Langmore's lawyer."

"Hold up on that, Dom," Baseball Cap Guy said.

"I'm sorry. Is Mrs. Langmore expecting you?" My gaze drifted to the main house that had sat eerily still since my arrival.

Phone Guy lifted an eyebrow and smirked, his self-importance on full display. Baseball Cap Guy held up his hand effectively silencing his companion and smiled. What I could see of his face transformed, and I found myself lowering my gaze as a different kind of heat sparked in my cheeks. "We'll come back later. Sorry to bother you." Baseball Cap Guy removed his hat, dragged his fingers through his thick brown hair, then settled the hat back down on his head, never taking his dark brown eyes from my face. His whiskered jaw suited him.

And me.

A flash of memory slammed into me. *Those eyes. Those eyes.* I recognized those eyes. Tall, muscular, well-built, former hockey star Nicholas Moretti. He graduated with me from Walleye High. Same year. We traveled in completely different circles. Correction: he had a circle of friends surrounding him.

I was a solitary figure moving through high school, counting the days until graduation.

What is Nicholas doing at Mrs. Langmore's home?

"Did you have an appointment with Mrs. Langmore?" I asked, dipping my head and tucking a strand of hair behind my ear. Did he recognize me? *Fat chance.*

"No," the man Nicholas referred to as Dom said, an edge to his tone. "Do *you* have one?" His beady eyes flashed annoyance, as if I was somehow his competition. What was going on here?

I glanced toward the front door. The house remained quiet. My grandmother managed this property, and it didn't seem likely that the elderly Mrs. Langmore was going to fill in during her absence. She had employees for a reason. Feeling oddly protective of Mrs. Langmore, I said, "Perhaps I can take a message." Without waiting for a reply, I grabbed my boyfriend bag from the ground and slung it over my shoulder, growing weary of the self-important guy and hoping I conveyed my impatience.

"Are you family?" Nicholas asked hesitantly. He obviously didn't recognize me. Why would he? He didn't know I existed in high school. And I liked to think I didn't resemble the quiet girl who wore castoffs from Goodwill.

"No, but I'm more than capable of taking a message." I ran a hand across the back of my neck.

"If you're not family, what are you doing here?" Dom seemed to be growing more suspicious which set my nerves on edge.

"If you must know, my grandmother works for Mrs. Langmore. She manages the property and lives in the bungalow out back." I gestured with my thumb in the general direction of the lake. I wasn't pleased with their appearance—for whatever reason—but I was more comfortable being forthcoming now that I knew they weren't axe murderers. Unless my former classmate had a dark side.

Dom's face registered a hint of surprise before his eyes grew steely. "Your grandmother is going to have to look for a new job."

Nicholas sighed, and his shoulders fell. "Don't mind my brother. His favorite pastime is being an ass."

Ah, brothers.

"What the—?" Dom shook his head, then turned away to take a call. He apparently had more important people to deal with.

A knot hardened in my stomach. "What did your brother mean by that?" Had Mrs. Langmore already replaced her grandmother after her stroke, to care for this huge property? No, that didn't seem right.

"Like I said, my brother is a jerk. Don't listen to him." Nicholas offered his hand. "I'm Nicholas Moretti."

"Oh." I accepted his outstretched hand. "Elizabeth." I held my breath, waiting to see if he was going to ask if I was the nerd who spent my afternoons in the school library. Maybe *he'd* apologize for being the jerk when he ignored me back then because he obviously couldn't resist me now after my glow up. This had the potential to play out like one of those romantic movies where the second-chance lovers reunite. Or maybe opposites attract. A million tropes bounced around my brain.

Nicholas jerked his chin toward the bag slung over my shoulder. "Are you coming or going?"

"Arriving," I muttered, glad he couldn't read my mind.

"You said your grandmother works for Mrs. Langmore." A shadow raced across the depths of his brown eyes. "Didn't she tell you?"

My heart dropped and I second-guessed that breakfast burrito I had wolfed down on my drive into town. "No." The fact that he didn't recognize me seemed inconsequential now. "Tell me what?" His reticence was getting on my nerves.

Dom hollered, "She's in hospice," in the same tone he

might have used to tell the barista she had gotten his order wrong.

"Oh…that's news to me." I grew dizzy. "Mrs. Langmore has always been so kind to my family. I'm sorry to hear that. I'll have to stop by and visit her. Is she here in town?" My thoughts spilled out in a barrage of questions.

"I believe so." Nicholas had his hands shoved in the front pockets of his jeans and he shrugged, an endearing gesture that made me question everything I thought I knew about the man.

A renewed sense of urgency pulsed through me as if I was standing next to an explosive that could blow at any minute. "I should go. Is there something you guys needed?"

To Nicholas's credit, he looked uncomfortable. "No, no, we can—"

"This house is sitting on five acres," Dom hollered over to his brother, perhaps relaying the information he was getting from his source on the phone. "A maid's quarters sits near the lake." He said a few indecipherable things then appeared to end the call. He strode over and offered his hand. "Dominic Moretti."

"Well, Dominic Moretti, I have things to do, and your brother decided you'd come back at another time."

Dominic shot his brother a side eye. "Perhaps…" He started to reach for something in his back pocket, but his phone buzzed again and he swept his finger across the screen. I watched him, thinking, *Squirrel!* The man was easily distracted.

"Here." Nicholas handed over his business card. "We own Moretti Realty and Construction. We're interested in this property."

"I have nothing to do with that." I held the card between pinched fingers, as if accepting it was some sort of betrayal to Mrs. Langmore or my grandmother. Maybe both.

Nicholas took a step backward. "Hang on to it. Put in a

good word for us." He flashed a brilliant smile of perfect teeth. This Nicholas was the one I remembered. A smooth talker full of bravado. How easily I had almost been fooled.

Elizabeth sputtered. The audacity of these two men to come sniffing around a dear old woman's home. "When did you say Mrs. Langmore went into hospice?" The sharp edge to my words made it clear they had stoked a fire inside me.

Nicholas had the good sense to blush. "I'm not sure." He jerked his head toward his brother. "My brother heard about it. Wanted to check out the property."

Dominic lowered his phone. "Come on. We have another meeting."

Nicholas twisted his palms and shrugged as if to say *Sorry about that*, but if he was anything like he had been in high school, he lived his privileged life unapologetically.

Elizabeth watched the two men stroll to the road and step over the chain barrier. They appeared to exchange words with a woman passing by before getting into an expensive-looking SUV.

To my surprise, the woman turned up the driveway, slowed only briefly by the chain, making me wonder why Mrs. Langmore even bothered.

5 /

elizabeth

I debated jogging quickly away and disappearing into my grandmother's house before whoever this was could hassle me. Was it another real estate agent looking to land a huge commission, or one of the town's vultures swooping in to feast on an elderly woman's vast estate?

I was about to turn around and hightail it to the back of the property when I recognized Cassie Parker, the nurse from the ICU, and my blood ran cold.

Something has happened to Lin.

Pulse pounding in my ears, I instinctively glanced at my bag with my cell phone, wondering if I had missed a call. I clutched the strap slung on my shoulder and rushed toward Cassie. Forgetting a greeting, I blurted out, "Is everything okay?" I swallowed around a lump in my throat.

"Yeah, Lizzy, er...Elizabeth. Everything is fine. Sorry, didn't mean to scare you." A small smile touched the corners of her mouth.

I nodded and my shoulders sagged. "When I called the nurses' station this morning, they said no changes." My mind was still trying to catch up with the news that my grandmother hadn't taken a turn for the worst.

Cassie reached out and brushed my hand. "Your grandmother is awake. Awake but confused."

Hope made the sunlight breaking through the trees a little bit brighter. "Awake? They didn't..." My mind raced, trying to process this new information. "No one called me. That's good news."

"Someone will reach out, if they haven't already."

I fished in my bag and checked my phone. Sure enough, I had a missed call and voicemail. I tucked it away. "How is she?" My voice squeaked. I was so desperate for good news. "You said she's confused?"

"Confusion and memory issues are not unusual after a stroke. Her brain needs time to heal."

"Okay, okay. That's good that she's awake. I'll grab a few things and get up there." I glanced over my shoulder toward my grandmother's home, still trying to process everything. "Wait, I thought you were off today?"

"I stopped in to check on Linda." Cassie shrugged sheepishly. "Hazards of the job, I guess."

I tucked my chin, taken aback by my old friend's kindness. "Thank you."

"No worries. I usually go out for coffee, and your grandmother was on my mind." Cassie hoisted the paper cup in her hand. "If I had known you were here, I would have brought you some."

"Ha." Suddenly my bladder reminded me of the large double-double I had consumed on the drive in from Buffalo. I furrowed my brow. "Were you coming here to check on my grandmother's house?"

"Linda was agitated about her dog. I promised I'd come feed him."

"Her dog?" I pinched the bridge of my nose.

"Yeah, she was worried about Henry."

I blinked slowly. "As a child she had a dog named Henry."

Cassie shrugged. "Mind if I come in so I can reassure her? I can grab some of her personal items while I'm here."

"Sure. Maybe we'll both be surprised." I laughed, somewhat embarrassed. Maybe Lin had gotten a new pup in the years since I last visited, but I doubted it. Lin didn't like to be tied down to pets or kids. And there'd be no reason to keep it a secret. "Come on, I'll show you the house." The dried grass crunched under our feet as we crossed the field to Lin's bungalow.

"Any idea when she'll be released?" My question was premature, but I was hungry for information, any information.

"A patient makes gradual improvements after a stroke. Usually by the twenty-four-month mark, that is as far as they're likely to improve." Cassie's footsteps kept pace with mine.

Two years.

I froze and turned around. "Two years?"

Cassie must have read the panic in my eyes because she added, "Her body and mind have to heal and that takes time. She's strong." Seemed nurse Cassie was a lot more nurturing and sympathetic than twelve-year-old mean-girl Cassie.

This thoughtful woman had come all this way to check on a patient's childhood dog because she was genuinely a nice person. Apparently people did change.

"You never left Walleye Point?" I asked.

"Got my nursing degree in Buffalo and decided to come back. I like working in the community I grew up in."

A regular saint. I hated that I was being petty, but this place brought it out in me.

When we reached the front of Lin's bungalow, I frowned at the unkempt garden. Dead leaves were trapped in the dried stalks that swayed in the stiff lake breeze. It was such a disorienting sight that I half expected to see a hungry puppy come tearing toward us.

"It looks like she hasn't been able to take care of the property for a while," I muttered. There was no other explanation. My grandmother was house-proud and took great care of the entire estate. The tall grass brushed my calves as my blood thrummed loudly in my ears. "Maybe she hadn't been feeling well."

"Did she complain of headaches, fatigue?" Cassie asked, following my lead through the trampled grass. "Mood changes?"

I frowned but didn't turn around. "I hadn't talked to her in a few weeks." I was being generous. It had been longer for sure. I couldn't remember the last time I had been home. This garden was usually cut back for winter in late fall. It was April. My eyes burned with shame, and I was grateful I could blame the tears on the brisk wind.

Around the front of my grandmother's home facing the lake, I picked up a plastic watering can and set it on the step. Nausea roiled in my belly as I took in the scene. It appeared that the porch had been used as a storage area of sorts. I grabbed the banister at the base of the steps to steady myself. I turned my palm over to find speckles of white paint chips. The single-story bungalow had seen better days. I closed my eyes, fearing the complete stillness meant I was about to faint.

"Liz…Elizabeth, are you okay?" Cassie placed her hand on my arm.

"I can't imagine why Lin let things get so bad." The earthy scent of Lake Erie after a cold winter reached my nose. April had always been a month of transition. One day it could be sleeting, and the next, warm with the promise of summer and days spent on the glider with a bowl of popcorn and lemon iced tea, reading Stephanie Meyer and Suzanne Collins until the sun set and I couldn't see the words on the page.

"All this stuff wasn't here before?" Cassie said the word "stuff" like it had a bad taste. Or maybe I was projecting.

"No." Stacked cardboard boxes, most damp and crushed,

beach chairs, umbrellas, empty plastic nursery trays...I blinked rapidly, wishing it would all go away, including my former classmate.

"How did she get in and out of the house? There's no access." Cassie picked up a rusted garden tool. I felt an irrational protective urge and yanked the tool from the woman's hand.

"There's a side entrance. Maybe she uses that." I pushed aside a box with my foot and sat down on the steps. The wood planks sagged under my weight. "My grandma still lives here, doesn't she?" Shame heated my face at having to ask this question, but that could be the only logical answer. My grandmother would never live like this.

"This is the address on her license." Cassie planted her hands on her hips, a woman devising a plan.

But I didn't want her making any decisions when it came to *my* grandmother. I didn't want a stranger doing nice things for *my* family. Like, who came all this way on their day off for a patient?

I clenched my jaw, realizing I was being totally irrational. Maybe it was the shock of this unbelievable mess.

A dog would be barking like crazy if it existed, right? I grabbed the railing and pulled myself up. "Well, I don't see a dog. You did your duty." I cleared my throat. "Go enjoy your day off." I hated my dismissive tone, but I was so frustrated and Cassie happened to be the only one here.

"Can I grab a few of her things?" Cassie asked, seemingly not affected by my curt tone.

"You wait here." A familiar blue flowerpot sat on the bottom step with dead geraniums. I tilted it and discovered the key. *Thank goodness for small favors.* "I'll go to the other door." The key worked in both locks.

Leaving the ever-so-helpful nurse at the front of the house that faced the lake, I walked around to the side entrance, where my step-grandfather used to park his motorcycle before he roared off, claiming he hadn't signed up to raise a snot-nosed kid. Initially, I had been thrilled the nasty man was gone, until my grandmother started blaming me for his absence.

Being back here elicited memories from my tumultuous teenage years. But never in the six years that I lived with my grandmother had there been heaps and heaps of things piled everywhere. The colors, the shapes, the sizes, the smells. Sensory overload.

Breathing shallowly, I navigated my way, clearing an area in front of the door as best I could. I yanked on the screen door, the bottom edge shredding yellowed newspapers as I pried it open just enough to slip through. Stale air floated out from the kitchen. I stepped over and around things in my way.

"What in the world?" I muttered to myself. "How did you live like this, Lin?"

I maneuvered around piles and piles of personal effects, my footing unsteady. I hated to think what that squishy feeling underfoot was. In the kitchen, dirty bowls sat nestled one inside another, ready to tip over if not for all the other stuff propping them up. In the family room, the TV screen was blocked by Target and Wegman's bags, the plastic ones. This had been going on for a long time—New York State had outlawed plastic bags years ago. I moved deeper into the house, sidestepping every imaginable thing. Unsuccessfully. I tried not to imagine what might be under there.

Definitely no dog, at least not one that was waiting to be fed.

A soft groan made me turn. Cassie stood in the doorway between the kitchen and family room holding the back of her sleeve to her nose.

"I had no idea," I said, feeling like the piles around me were about to bury me. Maybe they would swallow me up and spare me this excruciating embarrassment.

"It's a mess," Cassie said unhelpfully.

"You think?" I snapped. I hated feeling petty, but this situation reminded me of the awkward teenager I had been.

Cassie's pale eyebrow arched, then she smoothed her expression. "I can provide names of resources. Social workers who can help you and your grandmother." Cassie's voice was muffled under the sleeve of a sweatshirt held to her mouth and nose. She was tearing up and nearly gagging and even then she didn't snap back at me. It was hard to believe Cassie was the same person who humiliated me as a child.

It had been Cassie's thirteenth birthday, a slumber party. I was the new girl and had been excited to be included. The girls had stayed up later than *Saturday Night Live* and whatever silly show came on after that. It was then that Ashley Morris, Cassie's BFF since kindergarten, started a chant about Lizzy Borden. I had gone by Lizzy back then, and kids made the dumbest connections to taunt the weakest link. It had been especially cruel because my mother had died. Certainly not by forty whacks, but still. As an adult, I could rationalize that the meanness stemmed from jealousy, fear that Cassie had made a new friend. Ashley worried she'd be the odd man out. But young me had been devastated. These girls had been awful to me.

I pressed the heel of my hands to my eyes and groaned, clearly overwhelmed. Cassie's voice grew distant, then close, then distant again.

I am not going to pass out.

I lowered my hands and focused intently on the nurse's words that sounded like they were coming from the far end of a tunnel: "Linda can't come home to this."

6 /
nicholas

I should have driven myself.

I grabbed the *oh-shoot-we're-gonna-crash* handle on my brother's SUV and gritted my teeth. Telling Dominic to slow down or take it easy on the corners would only egg him on. Dominic drove with the hubris of someone who thought he was immortal. His darn phone was more important than the fast-approaching bumper of the SUV slowing down ahead of us. In the passenger seat, I stomped my foot on the imaginary brake.

Dominic swerved, palm on the steering wheel, all casual, into a parking spot conveniently located in front of the law offices on Bay Street. My older brother laughed. "You are such a wimp."

I resisted taking the bait. I might be twenty-eight, but my brothers liked to give me the equivalent of a headlock and a noogie every chance they got. They treated me as if I was inferior. But the big difference between little Nicky and adult Nicholas was that I no longer reacted, not outwardly anyway. It had taken countless beatings and verbal assaults as a kid to learn that to react was to ask for it.

Except for the occasional passenger-side brake. I couldn't help that.

And our father goaded us on. I was the youngest and Junior had warned me to toughen up because people only picked on the weak. Sounded like bully training to me.

Ultimately, I had grown to not really care, not in the same way I had as a little boy determined to earn my half-brothers' acceptance. Now it was just annoying, a waste of time. Mostly, I was cool as ice. The Italian Ice had been my nickname since becoming a high school hockey standout. I now trained my intense focus on new ambitions while keeping my brothers close when necessary, with plans to shut them down eventually—crush them—and prove once and for all that our father had underestimated the youngest Moretti.

I was no one's punching bag.

I had lost all respect for my philandering oldest brother, Sal, and my condescending middle sibling, Dom. Both would be liabilities in our father's company. Our father couldn't see it. Yet. I had to prove I was worthy of the old man's absolute trust, and Dominic—wittingly or not—had just handed me the inside track on making one of my father's biggest dreams a reality: a boutique hotel on a prime piece of real estate overlooking Lake Erie. Right in the heart of Walleye Point.

If I could break ground on the hotel and event center and turn a profit in the first year, I'd kick aside the shackles anchoring me to my brothers. And my father, who would leave me alone to continue making the entire Moretti family wealthy.

Wealthier.

I'd no longer be a failure in my father's eyes.

When Dom and I entered the lawyer's lobby, the young man sitting at the receptionist's desk told us that Mrs. Langmore's lawyer, Peter Shipley, was on a call and would be with us shortly. I saw this as an opportunity to get rid of Dominic.

"I'll wait to speak with Mr. Shipley. Go on and meet Diane for her appointment."

Dominic raised an eyebrow while still engrossed in his

cellphone. "I have some time. Let me make the introductions. Ship is an old friend." My brother claimed to have many old friends, all of them with ridiculous nicknames.

"Much appreciated," I said, blowing smoke up my brother's backside.

"Can't build the lakefront hotel without lakefront property," Dominic muttered under his breath as he furiously typed on his phone. After a few swipes, he looked up. "Where is this guy?"

As if summoned, an older man in a well-tailored suit appeared, rushing to greet us. "Hello, Dom. How are you, man?" The lawyer shook my brother's hand and patted him on the elbow like they were old pals.

Dominic gestured with his head toward me. "My little brother, this is Peter Shipley."

Little brother. Dom is such a jerk. I extended my hand. "Nicholas Moretti, nice to meet you."

Mr. Shipley reached out with a fist, and I closed my palm to give him a quick fist bump instead. Once inside his office, the lawyer motioned to two leather chairs in front of a large wooden desk cluttered with books, files, and papers. Hopefully his business dealings were more organized than his office. The lawyer sat down and picked up a pen, fidgeting with it between his fingers.

I glanced at Dominic who had finally placed his phone face down on his thigh. Before my brother had a chance to commandeer the meeting, I spoke up. "I understand you represent Mrs. Langmore's estate."

Mr. Shipley slotted the pen into a SUNY Buffalo Law School mug that held a bunch of number two pencils and yellow highlighters. "You Morettis don't waste time." He folded his hands and placed them on top of a legal pad covered in doodles with crumpled edges, his expression growing more serious. "I agreed to this meeting because Dom and I are old golfing buddies. But you do realize that woman is not deceased. She has simply relocated."

"Of course, of course," Dominic said before discreetly checking his phone, which was hidden from the lawyer's view by the desk. "We'd like to make an offer. Save her the hassle of listing the property."

The lawyer adjusted the yellow-lined pad, aligning it with the paper blotter on his desk. "I value my client's privacy." He cleared his throat. "All I can say is that the property is not currently for sale. Beverly Langmore has a deep attachment to her home. It's been in her family for generations. Her grandfather built it as a summer residence after achieving success in the steel industry."

"It's sitting empty. Wouldn't she like to see it come to life again?" Dom asked, his voice seeming too loud for the small space.

Ship gave his old friend a sly smile. "I imagine she wouldn't like to see her beautiful home bulldozed for whatever you're planning."

A niggling of discomfort made me shift in my seat. "Does she have family she plans to leave it to?" Even as the question slipped past my lips, I sensed the ickiness of it. Perhaps in trying to break from my father and brothers, I was becoming more like them.

The lawyer dipped his head and studied the surface in front of him, as if debating something. Then he turned his attention to me. "She's left her entire property to Mrs. Linda Graham."

"Who?" If Dominic opened his eyes any wider and kept blinking he'd turn into an owl.

"Mrs. Langmore's cleaning lady, or at least that's how their relationship started. Over the years, Mrs. Graham took on more and more responsibilities. She appears to manage the entire property, keeping it up and all. Mrs. Langmore is very fond of her. She made her plans clear in the will."

"Wow. The whole thing?" Dominic sat up straight, then crossed his arms over his broad chest. "No family, huh?"

"Nope. Mrs. Langmore was an only child who never married." The lawyer snatched the pen from the UB mug and started bouncing it again on the back of his knuckles.

The young woman we had met at the Langmore's earlier today came to mind. She was headed to her grandmother's home. "Mrs. Graham lives on the property?" I suspected I already knew the answer.

"As far as I recall, she lives in the servants' quarters by the lake. Not sure if that has changed since I last saw Mrs. Langmore."

"How long ago was that?" Dominic asked, his words slow, as if he were putting plan B together.

Mr. Shipley lifted the cover of a folder, checked something, then slapped it closed again. "A few months ago. We made some minor tweaks to her will before she moved."

"Was she of sound mind?" Dominic asked. "She's pretty old, right? A question could be made."

I fisted my hands, then forced myself to relax. Dominic had zero chill.

Mr. Shipley hesitated for a fraction, then cleared his throat. "Mrs. Langmore is sharp. I've known Beverly for my entire life. My father represented her before I did. She knows what she wants." A beat of silence stretched between us. "The will stipulates that Mrs. Graham is not to be notified of her inheritance until after Mrs. Langmore's passing. She was adamant about that."

"Maybe we can convince Mrs. Langmore to sell it to us first," Dominic said, raising a dark eyebrow. When we were younger, it had been a unibrow. "Perhaps Mrs. Graham would find a monetary windfall more desirable than a money pit."

The color drained from Shipley's face, as if only now

considering his ethical breach. "You cannot tell Mrs. Langmore or Mrs. Graham that you talked to me. Understood?"

"Of course," Dom said in the same tone he used when his wife asked him to do a chore that he had no plans of doing.

I stood and shook the lawyer's hand. "Thank you for your time."

Once back in the car, Dominic turned on the ignition, then glanced over and made a sucking sound with his teeth. "Sounds like you have a challenge on your hands."

"How's that?" I asked, trying to shake off the second-hand embarrassment served up by my brother's lack of self-awareness.

"Mrs. Langmore ain't gonna last long. When she goes to the great beyond, the housekeeper gets the land." Dom pointed at me aggressively. "You need to be the first person that Graham woman calls when she's looking to sell. Swoop in to make her an offer before she realizes what she's sitting on. I bet you could get an 'in' with the granddaughter. I saw the way she was looking at you. I'd do it myself, but…" He hitched his lip in a snarl, as if having a wife could be a real inconvenience sometimes.

I rolled my eyes. Somehow, I doubted even the pesky detail of being married would stop my brother from trying to gain leverage with a beautiful woman if it meant money in his pocket. However, Dom was flying down to Florida tomorrow for a golf tournament. So, that left me to find an angle to be first in line to buy the Langmore property.

I clicked my seatbelt in place. There had to be another way.

"Did you know that chick?" Dom asked, clearly not willing to drop it.

I slowly shook my head. Something niggled at me. *Did I?* "No, I don't think so." And that was the truth.

"Maybe it's time to get to know her. Wouldn't be much of a sacrifice. She's pretty hot."

"I'm not going to use her." I liked to think I wasn't like the rest of the Moretti men.

Dominic scoffed. "You will never make it in this business." He pumped his fist. "You have to be aggressive. Use any and all advantage." Dom's phone dinged, eliciting an under-the-breath curse. "My flight tomorrow got canceled." He did a quick check of his mirrors before pulling out into traffic on Bay Street. "I'm gonna see if I can reschedule my flight for tonight."

"Hold up," I said, planting my hand on the dash. "Drop me off here. I can walk to the office."

"Whatever." Dominic pulled over, parallel to another car, his impatience radiating off him. "Nicky boy, I know you want to prove to Daddy that you have what it takes…" He leaned closer and lifted a thick eyebrow, a knowing smile slanting his thin lips. "This is the deal. This is the one."

Ignoring my brother's lukewarm pep talk, I said, "Safe travels," before slamming the door. I didn't need my brother telling me anything. I had what it took, and I'd prove it. On my own terms.

I was done letting my father down.

And myself.

elizabeth

I stood by my grandmother's hospital bed, willing her to open her eyes. "She was awake earlier?" I whispered, unable to hide the desperation in my voice. "Talking?"

"Yes," Cassie said. "She's going to need her rest." She adjusted the edge of the blanket. "Have you had anything to eat?"

My old friend had kindly offered to come with me to the hospital, but I couldn't rightly take up all of her time. "I'm not hungry." Any thoughts of food had gone poof when I had gotten a whiff of Lin's musty, stale house.

"You need to eat. Something light anyway."

"Yeah, maybe later," I said noncommittally.

"If you don't mind, I have some other errands to run." Cassie gently touched my arm, as if seeking permission to leave. "Linda is being well cared for here."

"Of course, thank you for everything."

Cassie turned to leave, then paused. "It's nice to see you. I'm sorry it's under these circumstances." She dragged her lower lip through her teeth. "I always felt crummy that we had a falling out when we were kids."

"That was a lifetime ago," I said distractedly.

"I think about how mean we were to you at that slumber

party." Cassie's face flushed pink. "I should have been a better friend."

Despite my denial, that night had been a core memory. One that added to my distrust of relationships. "We were kids." I smiled, genuinely this time. "You've more than made up for it by taking such good care of my grandmother." I meant that. I had been a kid, but so had Cassie. Mistakes were made.

Cassie shrugged shyly. "That's my job."

"You've done far more than your job requires, and I appreciate it. I know Lin does too."

Cassie placed a finger over her lips. "Don't tell the others." She tipped her head toward the door. "I gotta go. You good?"

"We'll be fine."

"Oh, I meant to tell you, once they discharge Linda from the hospital, she'll go to rehab for a few weeks. Then, of course, there's the issue of her house."

I looked up at the tiled ceiling and softly groaned. "One step at a time, right?" Man, I was the queen of clichés today. What *else* could I say? The mess at the house would have to be dealt with.

"Let me know how I can help. I do have resources." This hadn't been the first time Cassie had offered assistance. How would Lin feel about that? Outsiders knowing her business.

"Thank you."

"You're welcome. Well, you know where to reach me if you need anything."

I kept my grandmother company for a while until the list of things bouncing around my head made me antsy. I patted Lin's hand. "I'll be back later."

Once outside the hospital, I gulped in a lungful of crisp spring air. The temperatures had warmed to the mid-sixties. Heavenly after the rough winter we'd had.

I dropped off my rental car and took an Uber to the house and grabbed Lin's car keys. My grandmother's old beater would suffice to get me around town. I'd need to save my money for a hotel now that my grandmother's place was uninhabitable.

I found the Walleye Point Lakeside Inn just west of the center of town. Once I paid for a couple nights and checked into my room, I realized "lakeside" wasn't the only exaggeration on the sign out front. *Clean* and *updated* were also a stretch. The room smelled of stale cigarette smoke and something else that I didn't allow myself to think about.

Shuddering, I pressed the back of my hand against my nose, inhaling the lavender lotion I had splurged on once I had a big-girl job. I wasn't high maintenance, but…ugh…

Be grateful there's no clutter.

I wouldn't be inclined to get too cozy here. More incentive to clean up the house.

Unable to stay in the dingy room a moment longer, I walked into town. A briny smell floated in on a steady breeze. When I first came here as a kid, I was in awe of the lake. The beautiful view had buoyed my spirits after my mother's death. But Lin's unhappiness about raising her granddaughter had been palpable, sinking me back into a dark depression.

Shaking away the unhappy memories, I focused my attention on what I loved about Walleye Point. The deep lawns of beautiful lakefront homes gave way to quaint shops and restaurants, most of them still closed for the season or only open for limited hours. I wasn't sure where I'd grab something to eat. Most of the businesses were unfamiliar to me. It wasn't like we had been in the habit of eating out when I grew up here. We never had any money.

A few restaurants, a bakery, and a couple takeout joints were sprinkled between the bookstore, tailor, and an electronic repair shop that probably didn't have enough business to stay open for more than a few hours a day.

The door of a restaurant with a bold red awning swung

open, and a man emerged carrying takeout boxes, nearly running into me. My stomach growled. I grabbed the handle and slid inside. A casually dressed teenager rushed past, telling me to grab a seat wherever. I chose one of the booths overlooking the choppy waters of Lake Erie.

I'd never grow tired of this view.

The same harried young woman with a purple streak in her blonde hair and a gold nose ring came by with a couple of menus and set them down on the table in front of me. I wished I had been as confident as this woman appeared to be when I was younger. Instead of trendy and chic, I went for "blend in and avoid getting noticed."

"Waiting for someone." It was more a statement than a question.

"Just me."

Purple Streak snagged the extra menu. "Do you need time to decide?"

I glanced down quickly. "The beer-battered fish fry, please."

"Fries and coleslaw?"

"Absolutely. And water to drink is fine."

The woman smiled brightly and met my gaze. In that moment, I realized she was older than I had initially thought. Mid-twenties maybe. Not a teenager. "Perfect. I'm Aggie if you need anything."

"Thanks, Aggie." I turned and stared out over the water again. In a few weeks, it would be filled with all kinds of boats, kayaks, and Ski-Doos. I used to sit on my porch and watch them speed by. Sometimes my high school classmates would race by in a boat with a slew of friends bouncing and squealing in delight on an inner tube in tow. Others enjoying the lake were mostly the summer people.

My grandmother knew which kids came from good families and which ones were trouble. Before Lin took the job full-time with Mrs. Langmore—before I had lost my mother and moved to Walleye Point—she had worked for many of their families. "The richer ones are the worst," Lin used to say. When the golden kids zipped by on their Ski-Doos, she'd encourage me to get my nose out of the book and go down to the beach. Invite them up for a soda. *As if.* When the sketchy ones (Lin's words) lingered at the corner store with vapes in their fists, she'd mutter something about those being her daughter Jennifer's kind of friends, the insinuation being that I had better steer clear. It always pained me that Lin spoke so dismissively of her dead daughter. My mom.

Maybe that was my grandmother's coping mechanism. Anger might be easier to hold onto than devastating grief.

Lin was a firm believer in the adage, "if you made your bed, you darn well better lie in it." No take backs. No sympathy for when your life was a mess and you were dying of cancer. It seemed needlessly cruel to me. However, I had been grateful to be spared from foster care.

A muffled buzz snapped me out of my reverie. My cell phone. I dug into my purse to find it. *Malissa Turner.* FaceTime.

I accepted the call with a quiet voice. "Hey there." Even though the restaurant was practically empty, I didn't want to be one of *those* people who spoke loudly and completely obliviously in a public setting.

My college roommate was calling from her office in Boston. A splash of red from her suit coat hanging on the back of her desk chair was in sharp contrast to her white blouse. Her impeccable makeup and hair made me feel like a slug in the small image of myself in the corner of the screen. I ran a hand self-consciously across my frizzy halo. I hadn't taken much care in getting ready, only applying lip gloss and a little mascara. Heat licked my pale cheeks. *Oh no.* I must have looked like a complete mess when I met Nicholas this morning. *Ugh.*

"It's a nice day in Boston," I said. Behind my friend, the bright sun reflected off a glass high-rise building.

Ah, I miss my favorite city.

Malissa glanced over her shoulder as if she needed to double-check the view from her window. These big architectural firms had some great perks but worked their employees to the bone. I wasn't sure if it was worth the trade-off, but my friend still had a job while I didn't.

"Every day feels the same." Malissa laughed, acting aggrieved, but she loved her job. She worked for a top Boston architectural firm that apparently hadn't been affected by the downturn in the economy. Malissa pressed her lips together and frowned. "Sorry about that."

"No worries. It was probably a blessing in disguise, all things considered." I had been texting Malissa with updates about my grandmother. Malissa had been my first true friend, one who didn't judge me based on my past, and one I could trust. Truly trust. I was grateful that technology allowed us to continue our friendship despite the miles. I had already lost too much.

"How is Lin doing?" Malissa knew my grandmother as well as anyone. Even though Malissa had never been to Wall-eye, we shared everything in late-night gabfests over cheap wine and nachos.

"Same, but they assure me things will get better. Something about taking time."

"That's good." Malissa looked up and accepted a piece of paper from someone offscreen. "I wish I could fly out there and be with you."

I could hear muffled voices in the background. Malissa was, after all, in her office during a workday. "Do you have to go?" I didn't want to hold her up.

"Big presentation. I have a few more minutes, though."

I decided now was not the time to share the horrid conditions Lin had been living in. A familiar shame heated my cheeks. *I should have come back to Walleye Point sooner. Maybe I could have seen the signs. Stopped the hoarding before it got out of control.*

Malissa would mean well, but her practical advice—from her worldview of an uncomplicated life of long hours, normal boyfriend, normal parents—might annoy me a smidge, and only because I loved her. Otherwise it would have frustrated me a lot.

"You okay?" Malissa asked. I couldn't hide anything from her.

"Tired. That's all." I placed the palm of my hand over the utensils and slid them closer to me.

"Excuse me," a male voice said, approaching from behind. On the screen, a miniature Nicholas Moretti came into view and I spun around. "Oh, I'm sorry," he said. "I didn't realize you were on a call."

My pulse thrummed in my ears, and I squeaked, "It's okay. I'll be done in a minute."

Nicholas held up his hand in an apologetic gesture. I waited a beat until he walked away. "Sorry about that. Hold on." I dug into my purse and put in my EarPods. "What were we talking about?" My brain had gone completely blank.

Malissa leaned into the camera, her perfectly lined lips whispering, "Who was that?"

I cut my gaze to a nearby table where Nicholas had retreated. Thank goodness I had put in earphones. "Um..."

Malissa tapped the pads of her fingers together and smiled. "There's a story there. For later." She planted her hands on the desk. "Gotta go. I expect to get a full update later." She blew a kiss that would have seemed cheesy from anyone but Malissa.

"There's nothing—" Before I could finish that thought, the screen went blank.

Shaking my head, I removed my EarPods and pretended to study my phone. Nicholas could be heard chatting with the pretty waitress with a familiarity that suggested they knew each other.

Figures. Nicholas had been the prom king. The captain of the hockey team. The jerk probably didn't even peak in high school, I thought begrudgingly. I wished I had ordered take-out. Sitting here alone had reminded me of my days in middle and high school. Lunch period was the worst for loners like me. A familiar ache settled in my belly. How long would it take to clear out all the junk from Lin's house? Would my grandmother make a quick recovery? When could I bail? Get away from this small town.

How thoughtful of you.

Then another worry struck me: What if my grandmother got settled, only to have to move out because Mrs. Langmore sold the property? I made a mental note to visit the dear woman in hospice. I needed a solid plan.

My to-do list was growing longer than a CVS receipt.

Nicholas and the young waitress laughed, and I rolled my eyes. *What a charmer.* How annoying. He'd probably sweet-talk Mrs. Langmore into selling.

Shoot, shoot, shoot.

I'd have to get to her first—if I wasn't already too late—and convince Mrs. Langmore to hold off selling, at least not until Lin got her feet back on the ground. Lin would be devastated if she had to leave her lakefront bungalow. She had nowhere else to go.

Inwardly I groaned. I had to get my grandmother's home into shape. Lin and I didn't often see eye to eye, but I owed her this much for everything she had sacrificed for me.

nicholas

I leaned toward Elizabeth's table after she got off the phone. "Can I join you?" I gave her my best how-you-doing smile not sure what, if any, effect it would have on this seemingly serious woman.

She held out a welcoming palm and shrugged. I slid into the seat across from her before she could change her mind. "I hope you ordered the fish fry. Highly recommended."

"As a matter of fact, I did." She lined up the fork and knife and tilted her head, a quizzical look in her eyes imploring me to get on with it.

I glanced towards the door. "You seem to be distracted."

"No, just curious." She folded the edge of the napkin. "Are you here to tell me I need to pack up my grandmother because you've convinced Mrs. Langmore to sell the estate?"

I jerked my chin back, surprised by her directness. This woman had no idea that her grandmother would inherit everything when Mrs. Langmore died. But that could be tomorrow, or three years from now. The latter was unlikely if she was truly in hospice care. The lawyer hadn't mentioned her current health, however old age itself was terminal.

I quickly schooled my expression. "I'm not aware that the property is for sale." I wanted that land so badly that I could taste it. To prove I had what it took to succeed in my family's business.

"Here you go," my cousin Aggie said as she slid two fish fries in front of us. "You eating here?" she casually asked me, then swung her gaze to Elizabeth as if seeking confirmation.

Elizabeth shrugged. "Thanks for the food. Looks good."

"We're known for our fish fry." Aggie tucked the tips of her fingers into the white apron tied around her waist. "Can I get you anything else to drink?"

"I'll have whatever light ale you have on tap," I said.

"Make it two."

"Hold up," I said to my cousin, and the waitress paused, "this is my friend Elizabeth." Then to Elizabeth, I said, "This is my cousin, Aggie. Her mother runs this place. Best Italian restaurant in town."

Aggie rolled her eyes and pressed her fingers to the purple streak that was tucked neatly into a ponytail. "We're the *only* Italian restaurant in town."

Elizabeth laughed and something in my heart softened. "Nice to meet you."

"You, too." Aggie adjusted the apron fastened at her waist. "Are you from around here?"

"She's in town visiting family," I said, jumping in.

"Actually, I grew up here." A smile played at the corners of her pink lips.

I did a quick double-take and Aggie scoffed, clearly amused at my expense. "Your friend, huh?"

"You grew up here?" Maybe she was a few years younger than I was. That could explain why I didn't recognize her.

Elizabeth picked up her fork, flaked off some fish, and dipped it into the tartar sauce. She matched my cousin's energy with a coy smile. "I graduated with Nicholas."

I squirmed in my seat and wracked my brain. *That can't be right.* "You sure?" I would have remembered a face like hers —dark eyes, silky hair and porcelain skin. "No way."

Aggie shook her head. Amusement creased the corners of her eyes. "I'm going to leave you to figure this out while I see about your drinks." She spun around and disappeared behind a partition.

Elizabeth took another forkful of fish and tartar sauce but didn't lift it to her mouth. "I went by Lizzy back then. Lizzy Graham." Apparently she had decided to throw me a bone.

Lizzy. Lizzy. Lizzy. Do I know a Lizzy?

I squared my shoulders and pointed at her. "Of course." I was flat-out lying, and I suspected she knew it. "Lizzy." I studied her face. Still nothing registered. "And your grand-mother is Linda Graham." I wasn't sure why I was saying this out loud. It still didn't ring any bells.

She took a bite and lifted a perfectly groomed brow. Clearly she was done giving me hints. She placed her fist in front of her mouth as she chewed. "You don't remember me." Humor danced in her eyes. "It was a big school. Three hundred or so in our graduating class."

"I guess." I had no idea how big our class was. The only thing I knew for sure was that I had no recollection of this woman sitting across from me. Maybe she was mistaken. I casually pointed at her with my fork. "You graduated from high school in town? Walleye Point High School?"

"The one and only." She put another plop of tartar sauce on the crispy battered fish.

"You probably don't remember me either," I said, deciding to turn things around on her. It *had* been ten years.

Elizabeth tapped her chin with her index finger. "Hmmm…homecoming king. Star hockey player. Division One athlete." Her tone was sardonic. "Totally unforgettable."

"I can't believe I don't remember you." An idea started to tick in the back of my brain. Oh, maybe she was one of those brainy types, taking all the honors and accelerated classes. I considered myself smart enough, but I didn't stress about school. Turned out I didn't need ten APs to go to Notre Dame on an athletic scholarship, and my teachers tended to give me a pass because they liked the bragging rights that claiming the state championship in ice hockey provided. What a strange thing. I had been so puffed up as a kid that I hadn't been prepared for the failures that awaited me once I hit college.

"You really make a girl feel special." She smiled tightly, and light sparked in her eyes. Was she mocking me?

I studied her pink lips, wondering if they were as soft as they appeared.

"Well, I suppose I've completely botched this up." I pointed over my shoulder with my thumb. "Should I just go over there and leave you to eat your fish fry in peace? I've opened my mouth, inserted my foot." I waggled my eyebrows. "And this old sneaker is tough to chew." I laughed to hide my embarrassment. This woman wasn't cutting me any slack, and I wasn't used to that. A bashful smile and a wink usually got me out of all sorts of trouble. Not with the woman sitting across from me. Not a fan of self-recrimination—I had my older brothers to do that for me—I shifted my way of thinking. Perhaps I was being too tough on myself. I was a popular kid in high school. Everyone knew me. Was I expected to know everyone else in return?

You are truly a jerk. My self-importance seemed to know no bounds.

"Stay. Enjoy your meal," Elizabeth said, sounding unaffected. "Someone told me this place has the best Italian food."

"You're having fun at my expense, aren't you?" I wasn't used to women—at least one I was actively flirting with—subtly taking me down. Who was this Elizabeth—formerly known as Lizzy—Graham? I found myself eager to find out everything she had been up to in the ten years since we graduated.

"You have made it easy," she said, a flash of humor in her brown eyes.

"Not intentionally." I laughed at myself, feeling my shoulders relax.

"Don't feel bad. You've been a pleasant distraction. A badly needed one."

"Oh yeah?" Now I was really curious.

"My grandmother is in the hospital." She sighed softly.

"Oh, I didn't know," I said, feeling like a bigger jerk. *That's why she was in town.* "I'm sorry to hear that. Is she going to be okay?" The news that Linda Graham was the sole beneficiary of the Langmore estate came to mind. My father's dream of a boutique hotel on the lake was so close. My golden opportunity to prove I could be a success in his eyes— in my own eyes. I was tired of having the puck lined up perfectly and missing the shot. First by not graduating from college, then not getting drafted in the NHL, then being under the thumb of not only my father but my two older brothers.

This was my chance.

Which led me to wonder if something happened to Mrs. Graham, who would inherit the Langmore estate? All the options clicked through my brain, landing on the most obvious.

Was this beautiful woman next in line? Maybe she held the power of attorney for her grandmother. I scrubbed a hand across my face. I was such a ghoul. Apparently it was a Moretti trait—willing to do whatever it took to close the deal. I met Elizabeth's gaze and realized she had been saying something about a stroke and time.

Her grandmother.

"That's gotta be rough. Is there anything I can do?"

Elizabeth picked up a French fry. "Thanks, but I couldn't ask you for a favor."

"Why? We're old classmates."

The hint of humor in her eyes dimmed, replaced by a

cloud of worry. "You and your brother were checking out the Langmore place today. Is the property for sale?"

I held my best poker face. "As far as I know, it's not listed." Not a lie.

"I should visit Mrs. Langmore." Elizabeth pressed her lips into a flat line. "She was so good to both me and my grandmother." She took a bite of a fry then tossed it on her plate, as if thinking better of it. "I was sorry to learn she was in hospice."

Suddenly feeling the need to be completely honest, I confessed, "We—meaning my family and I—would love to buy the land when it does come up for sale."

Elizabeth's mouth formed a perfect O and she seemed stuck for a response. Disappointed maybe. "So my suspicions were right."

"Suspicions?"

"Why are you here?" Elizabeth met my gaze, her expression inscrutable. "You think I have some sway over Mrs. Langmore?"

"I don't mean to be insensitive, but someone is going to snatch up that property." For some reason, I sought her understanding. "My dad has always wanted to build a boutique hotel. It would be a perfect location. Good for the local economy."

Her gaze slid to the lake outside the wall of windows. "It is a pretty spot." Her voice grew soft. "Would you tear down the Langmore home?"

"It's in need of more TLC than we'd be willing to invest. New is better. Progress, right?" As soon as the words slipped out of my mouth, I realized she was not the intended audience for my flippant remark.

"Progress at the expense of preserving the past isn't always progress." Her steely gaze searched my face.

"We would make sure it fits the town's aesthetic." My father would have castigated me for my apologetic tone.

"It would be a shame to tear down the old house. They don't build them like that anymore," Elizabeth said. "The detail is amazing...and the craftsmanship." She waved her hand and drew in a deep breath. "Sorry, I get all wound up when it comes to architecture. It's my thing."

"Your thing?" I asked, eager to suss out more about her.

"I have a degree in architecture. I was working in Boston before..." She stumbled over her words, perhaps not wanting to share too much about herself. "Before I came here to help my grandmother recover."

I sensed she had skipped over an important detail. "You'll be going back to Boston? I mean once your grandmother gets better?" I found myself holding my breath, waiting for an answer.

She nodded almost imperceptibly. "Um, yeah, I hope so. Eventually. I love Boston."

Shame. I would have liked to get to know her. But maybe it would be easier to push my agenda if I wasn't looking at a romantic entanglement. I cleared my throat. "Are you staying on the property while you're in town?"

"No, I'm at the inn."

"The Walleye Point Lakeside Inn?"

She nodded.

"How's that old place?" I had hoped to lose my virginity to my prom date at the only motel in town until she got drunk and threw up in the back seat. I smelled puke for months afterward until I couldn't stand it anymore and traded the car in.

"I imagine it's the same as it's been for eighty years," she said, snapping me out of my momentary trip down memory lane. "Past its prime." She ran a finger across her lower lip. "Maybe your company can renovate that property. Tear that place down. Start new. You know, progress?"

This woman took my words and tossed them back at me.

"It's not lakefront," I said evenly. "Despite its aspirational name."

"True." She looked absentmindedly over my shoulder at something behind me, then reconnected her gaze with mine. She gave me a lopsided smile. Tough audience. "Maybe you could purchase nearby lake access," she suggested.

"People want the view."

"I get it. I love sitting by the lake." Elizabeth picked up a fry and dragged it through the ketchup, then held it up. "Here's hoping Mrs. Langmore lives a long time because she'll never agree to sell to developers, and I'd hate to see her beautiful home torn down."

I lifted my beer. "Here's to Mrs. Langmore." It seemed like the right thing to say.

She hoisted her drink. "To Mrs. Langmore."

I took a long swig, feeling like the world's worst human being. I set the glass down, rationalizing—it wasn't like I had any ill will toward the long-time Walleye-Point resident. No, I just needed to convince Mrs. Langmore to sell, or I'd have to wait out the inevitable.

Once the elderly woman passed, I'd have to persuade Elizabeth's grandmother to sell.

Yes, yes, I was the worst.

9 /
elizabeth

Early the next morning, I learned there was still no change in Lin's medical status. My grandmother mostly slept, with periods of confused wakefulness. Or something like that, according to the nurse who answered the phone when I called the hospital.

Satisfied she was stable, I headed from the inn to the bungalow on the Langmore estate. The sooner I cleaned it out, the sooner I could check out of the inn. I didn't want to spend any more of my limited resources. I had already traded my rental car for Lin's old Chevy. Even if money were no object, I was tired of stuffing my feet into sneakers whenever I rolled out of bed to use the bathroom. I didn't want to think about what might be ground into the 1980's royal blue motel carpet.

Not that Lin's place is going to be any better.

Once I arrived, I grabbed my Tim Horton's coffee and breakfast sandwich—I'd need the calories for this job—and headed to the picnic table, enjoying the view while I ate. The fresh lake air and books had saved me during my tumultuous teen years when I struggled to navigate the loss of my mom and the underlying resentment of my grandmother. I imagined my nonexistent therapist would tell me to cut off all ties. To protect myself. But my guilt was stronger. I'd get Lin back on her feet, then all bets were off.

Deciding I had stalled long enough, I balled up the trash and got down to the business of cleaning out my former home. I came prepared with large black garbage bags, rubber gloves, cleaning supplies, and a tall plastic tote. Despite slipping and sliding over magazines, newspapers, and heaven only knew what, I managed to bring the supplies in through the side door. I cleared a small spot in the kitchen, lined the garbage tote, and tossed anything that remotely resembled something that once passed for food or drink. Or anything that was in proximity or stuck to said food or drink.

I paused when I discovered a ceramic mug I had made in the seventh grade. *World's Favorite Mom.* "Grandmother" was too long, and I didn't feel like explaining myself. I wondered if schools had gotten any better at acknowledging during their Mother's Day festivities that some kids didn't have a mom. I tilted the mug and my stomach lurched at the sight of mold floating on top of a suspicious liquid.

How did you live like this, Lin?

Bile tickled the back of my throat and I had to take shallow breaths. *Mind over matter. I will not puke.* I tossed the entire mug and its contents into the trash. A bead of sweat rolled down between my shoulder blades. The stagnant air held an odor I feared was permanent. I leaned across the sink, careful not to brush against the dirty counter edge, and hoisted up the window facing Mrs. Langmore's house and the street beyond.

Despite the fresh breeze, I couldn't stem my growing nausea. I shoved the screen door, creating a small space to exit onto the porch. Staring past the mess, I focused on the murky lake and gray skies. A pair of gulls dipped toward the surface, then quickly caught some air and disappeared over the house.

Once I was convinced I wasn't going to hurl, I got to work

on the porch, tossing aside soft, water-damaged Amazon boxes and a plastic tote of baskets. So many baskets. I would have loved to sit on the glider and get lost in a book, forget about this mess. But if the glider was still here, it was buried under *So. Much. Stuff.*

My cell phone vibrated in my back pocket. I peeled off a glove and grabbed it. I was relieved to see it was a FaceTime call from Malissa and not the hospital.

Malissa squinted into the camera when I answered. "Where are you now?"

"At the house." When I first met my college roommate, I painted my lakeside life as idyllic, only revealing the truth once we established trust.

"Wow!" The heap of stuff loaded on the porch was visible behind me in the video call. "How is your grandma doing today?"

"As far as her stroke? Pretty much the same. As far as this?" I jabbed my thumb toward the house. "I had no idea she was a hoarder." That was the first time I had said the word out loud.

"Sorry I had no idea things were that bad. If I had…" Both knew Malissa's schedule was too jam-packed for her to come and help. "I'm sorry I didn't get back to you yesterday. I was swamped," Malissa said. "Apparently after providing exactly what the clients requested, they decided that's not what they wanted. I've been burning the midnight oil." She huffed in frustration.

Architects were used to that. In college, the architecture building's lights burned bright at all hours. Malissa and I would stroll back to our dorms after staying up all night, finishing projects minutes before they were due, our eyes gritty and heads pounding.

"I don't miss that," I said, staring over the lake with an unfocused gaze. I did miss the paycheck, though.

"You okay?" Malissa asked. "I'm worried about you. You

don't seem to be yourself. I guess it makes sense with every-thing going on."

I laughed, a high-pitched brittle sound. "I've been better, but I'll be fine." Being back here flooded me with a myriad of emotions. From the time I was eighteen, I had tried to forget this place.

"I wish I could get away and help. Work has been like herding cats lately."

"Don't give it another thought. I'll manage." I rested my elbow on the bottom post of the porch railing. "You have to see this." I pushed the button to turn the camera around.

"Fantastic," Malissa said, then sighed.

"If only I could get rid of *this* view." I flipped the camera back around and made a silly face, revealing the pile of junk behind me.

"Maybe that dude from yesterday can help."

"Who?" I knew full well who she meant. It was a game we'd play sometimes, pretending we were clueless, especially when it came to things we didn't want to discuss.

"The hot one at the restaurant." Malissa angled her head and pointed with two fingers at her eyes. *I saw you.* "Gotta love FaceTime."

"Just some guy I went to high school with." I rolled my eyes, as if the mention of him was ridiculous. "I'm not going to ask a practical stranger to help me clear out this mess." *I'd be mortified if he knew how my grandmother lived.*

"A stranger? Didn't you say you went to high school with him?" Malissa set down her pen, folded her arms, and stared intently into the camera. "This sounds like the setup for a meet cute."

"Ha. I thought you didn't have time to read for pleasure," I scoffed.

"Oh, I always make time." Malissa laughed. "Now seri-ously. Does hot guy have a name?" Malissa asked in true Malissa form.

"Nicholas Moretti."

"Did you guys date or something?"

"*Pfft.* We both know I didn't date anyone before he who shall not be named." Or after. Not really. I shuddered at the thought of Brian. An engineering major who was a sloppy kisser, not that I had anyone to compare his technique to. Despite his lack of skill in the romance department, I found myself falling for him. Maybe I had been too needy not to see him for what he was. I had a wake-up call when he stole one of my programming assignments. *Jerk.* I hated users. I was lucky the professor didn't call me out on the honor code. I could have lost my scholarship. My entire college career down the drain. To add insult to injury, he was cheating on me. After that, I swore off dating in college, deciding it was more fun to hang out with my girlfriends, like Malissa.

And less stressful.

"So...what's Nicholas Moretti's deal?" Malissa asked. "Is he married? He's married, right? That's what everyone does in a small town. Marries their high school sweetheart at a really young age. I've seen those Hallmark movies."

"OMG, stop." I laughed. Malissa's humor was truly good for the soul.

"Well...is he?" She propped the phone on her desk, keeping the camera focused squarely on her. She leaned over and grabbed a file from a drawer, then opened it.

"I..." I let out another breath. *Is he?* "How would Nathan feel about this line of questioning?" Malissa and Nathan had been dating for over a year now. Record length for popular and bubbly Malissa. Maybe getting older had mellowed her out.

"Nathan would agree you need to get some."

"Stop!" I dragged a hand through my hair as heat crept up my neck and cheeks. I found myself glancing around to make sure no one was within earshot. But of course there wasn't. I was fairly isolated out here. "He's interested in this property."

I pointed to the land in front of me, out of camera view. "His family runs a construction business and they want to build a hotel here."

"Is the house for sale?" Malissa asked. "You didn't mention that."

"That seems to be the million-dollar question. I'm going to have to talk to Mrs. Langmore. She recently moved to hospice, according to him." A mix of nostalgia and longing weighed on me. I had been doing my best to push those emotions aside. I had other things to focus on.

"What happens if this place gets sold out from under your grandmother? She'll be devastated." I was surprised by Malissa's concern. They mirrored mine. "I've watched some of those hoarder shows. She won't like it if you throw out her stuff. And without proper treatment, she's likely to fill up her house again."

I swiped the back of my jeans, feeling gritty. Cassie, the nurse at the hospital, had said the same thing about hoarders.

"I never pegged you for reality TV." I wished my friend would stop; she was stressing me out.

Malissa shrugged. "Mindless TV to decompress after work." She sighed. "I wish I was there to help you."

"Having someone to vent to has been a huge help." My stomach had settled and the knot between my shoulder blades had eased. "I better go. This place ain't gonna clean itself."

"You should get a dumpster. Might speed things up."

"Hmm." I had wondered how much garbage the town would take from the curb, not to mention how I'd get it all there. A dumpster was a good idea.

"I'm here if you need me. Supporting you from afar," Malissa said, her eyes tracking someone who had apparently entered her office.

"Thanks. Now get back to work."

"You too!"

I ended the call and stared out at the lake. What I wouldn't do to toss absolutely everything out and start fresh.

Kinda like in life.

Unfortunately, neither was possible.

10 /
elizabeth

A Google search and a quick phone call led me to room 109 at Oakwood Assisted Living. *Assisted living.* Not hospice. Sometimes the rumor mill got things a little jumbled. However, sadly, I wasn't sure it really mattered. When a person was Mrs. Langmore's age, time on this side of the dirt was limited.

The attendant at the front desk of the facility explained that Mrs. Langmore had been exceptionally tired of late but would gladly see me. The residents loved visitors, the woman explained, but apparently they were in short supply.

After signing in on the ledger splayed open on the desk—the last entry was two days ago—I followed the long hallway to a closed door with the number 109 and a placard with Beverly Langmore's name on it. A wave of tingles washed over me at the prospect of being reunited with the woman who had been so kind to me as a girl. *Why, oh why, did I stay away?* Blinking away my blurry vision, I took a breath and knocked. When no one answered, I twisted the knob and pushed the door open a fraction. "Hello, Mrs. Langmore. Hello," I called, wanting to give her a warning before I barged in.

A frail-looking Mrs. Langmore was sitting on a white couch, her head tipped back and her mouth open, asleep.

Hopefully.

I stepped into the room, my heart thundering in my chest. "Hello, Mrs. Langmore." My voice squeaked on the last syllable. Finding a dead Mrs. Langmore was not on today's bingo card.

The sweet woman lifted her head, and a rush of relief made me dizzy. *Thank goodness.*

Mrs. Langmore blinked a few times, as if orienting herself, and then a smile of recognition spread across her face. "Oh, come in, dear. Come in." She made to scoot to the edge of the sofa, then decided against it.

Her face was thinner and her eyes appeared rounder than what I remembered, but all in all she was still a woman who took care in her dress—linen pants and a white blouse with a purple brooch on her pretty cardigan.

Mrs. Langmore patted the cushion next to her. "Sit down, sit down. So nice to see you, dear."

I smiled, remembering how this sweet woman used to tell me to join her on the grass to garden so that she didn't have to strain her neck to look up at me. "How are you, Mrs. Langmore?"

"I haven't had a sick day in my life." She stroked my hand and, like years ago, I was struck by how the older woman's blue veins were visible through her translucent skin. "But I suppose you can't outrun time. How are you?"

"I'm fine." I paused for a minute. The elderly woman's greeting had been generically friendly, making me wonder if she recognized me. "Do you remember me?"

"Of course, Lizzy. It's been a long time." Mrs. Langmore studied me with bright blue eyes. "Are you still in..." she hesitated, as if trying to grab the thread of a memory, "... Boston. Yes, Boston."

"I was, but I've come back to Walleye Point for a bit." I

had decided not to upset Mrs. Langmore with news of Lin's stroke if she didn't already know.

"Linda must be so happy." A shadow flickered across her features at the mention of the woman who took care of her estate, then quickly disappeared. "Now I know what has kept your grandmother away. She usually brings me the mail from the house. I've missed her."

"Um…" I hesitated, then proceeded cautiously. "Lin is fine, but she is in the hospital." When the color drained from Mrs. Langmore's face, I gently took her hand. "The doctors assure me she'll be fine. She's recovering from a stroke."

"Oh, poor dear," Mrs. Langmore said, adjusting the crocheted blanket on her lap. "I was worried that the house would be too much for her to manage. I wanted to bring on more help, but she insisted she had it covered."

"Don't blame yourself. We both know how stubborn she can be." I forced a cheery tone. "She'll be fine. I'd be happy to bring your mail—that is, until my grandmother is up to it herself."

"That would be nice, dear." Mrs. Langmore studied my face thoughtfully. "It's remarkable how much you look like your mother." She shook her head. "Such a shame."

An icy knot twisted in my belly at the mention of my deceased mother. I was almost the age at which my mother had died. Refusing to entertain the morbid thought a moment longer, I said, "This place is nice." The suite was cozy and had a spark of Mrs. Langmore's style. I recognized a few pieces that had been brought from her estate, including a striped wing-backed chair with mahogany arms and a silver-framed black-and-white portrait of Mrs. Langmore's parents looking rather serious. As a kid, I used to stare at the old photos scattered around the mansion, wondering what was going on in the subjects' lives behind the split second captured in the image.

"It'll do. That big house got to be too much."

I returned my attention to my host. "It must have been a tough decision to move. You loved your home."

"You loved it too." A whisper of a smile touched the older woman's lips. "You begged and begged to go up onto the widow's walk."

Warm nostalgia made my skin tingle. "It is beautiful. It really is." I touched my cell phone absentmindedly, remembering how the old Victorian had recaptured my attention the moment I had returned to the estate a few days ago. "Would you mind if I posted some photos of the house on social media? On the internet."

My cheeks flared hot, feeling like I was intruding on something private and going against all of Lin's instructions to respect Mrs. Langmore's position as her employer. *The last thing I need is to lose this job now that I have one more mouth to feed.* No pressure, I remembered thinking at the ripe old age of twelve. As if moving in with my grandma after my mother's death had been my preferred life path.

"I wouldn't post anything personal, of course," I continued. "I'd like to highlight the beauty of the architecture. I'm sure people would love to see it."

Mrs. Langmore waved her hand. "I'm not sure what that all means...social media." She spoke the last two words slowly, as if trying them out. "I never did get dragged into the computer age, but if you mean you'd like to share photos of my home with the world, I'd love that. Very much." She drew in a deep breath through her nose. "My grandfather built that house. Brought in marble from Italy and tapestries from Asia. The Langmore name is synonymous with that home." The pride was evident in the woman's voice. Her shoulders straightened. "I only ask for one thing in exchange."

I tipped my head, waiting.

"I want to see the photos, too. Maybe print out some copies. We'll put them in frames." She held out her hand. "We could spruce this place up a bit."

Excitement bubbled in my chest. "It's a deal."

"Deal," Mrs. Langmore repeated, then plucked at a thread of yarn poking out from the blanket. "Thanks to Lin, I was able to stay home for far longer than I ever imagined. But once I fell and broke my hip, it seemed like the logical thing to move here after rehab." A spark lit her eyes as she gave a dramatic shudder. "The thought of navigating all those stairs makes me tired. And the staff here treats me well." She gave her head a quick nod, as if she had just decided something. "It's been a good move."

"I'm sorry you broke your hip, but I'm glad you found such a nice place," I said.

Mrs. Langmore shifted and patted my thigh. "It's time that we shared the beauty of Langmore."

"Of course. Thank you." Renewed enthusiasm for the project fluttered in my belly. This beautiful home had inspired my entire career. Such as it was.

"Are you staying at Lin's while you're here?" Mrs. Langmore asked.

My mind raced. Did Mrs. Langmore know about her tenant's hoarding habit? If not, I didn't feel it was my place to share. How would the elderly woman react if I told her I was staying at the inn? The inn had been a bit sketchy for years.

Before I had a chance to answer, Mrs. Langmore said, "Oh, Linda did mention she hasn't been very good about keeping the bungalow tidy." The woman waved her hand dismissively. "I imagine the poor dear was exhausted after cleaning my house. Who could blame her?" Mrs. Langmore extended an infinite amount of grace.

I listened with rapt attention. Did Mrs. Langmore know how truly out of hand Lin's "untidiness" had gotten?

"Linda has been so wonderful to me," Mrs. Langmore continued to praise my grandmother. "I suggested she move into the main house, but she said she liked her own space." She fingered the brooch on her sweater, as if trying to digest that. "I thought once I moved in here she'd finally take me up on my offer, but she said she doesn't know what she'd do with all that space. That she prefers the smaller home."

I suspected I knew the true reason. "We have always appreciated everything you've done for us. Lin wouldn't want to take advantage of your kindness."

"That's silly. Linda—and you—are family." She leaned in conspiratorially. "You'll have to convince her to move in, won't you? It's a shame for that house to stand empty." She lifted an eyebrow. "And if it's a little too drafty, or if the style is not to your tastes, maybe you could do updates. Take before and after photos. Share them with the world." Mrs. Langmore surprised me with a girlish giggle.

For someone who wasn't familiar with social media, Mrs. Langmore seemed like she'd be good at it. Home renovations were hot on all the current platforms. And renovations to a historic home would be serious clickbait.

Mrs. Langmore's eyes brightened. "*You* should stay at the house."

"Oh, I don't know..." Those were Lin's words coming out of my mouth. Inside, I was champing at the bit to get inside that old place and see what time had done to it. To explore with the knowledge I had garnered through my education and work. But would I be around long enough to make the updates Mrs. Langmore seemed so eager to have done?

Would Mrs. Langmore?

"Think about it, won't you?"

I nodded. "You're too generous."

"You were a determined young girl," the older woman continued. "You were enamored with that house. I am happy to share it with you." Mrs. Langmore had been the one to buy me a huge art pad and colored pencils when I showed an interest and upgraded my supplies as my skills improved. "I was always so tickled how excited you were to explore when you were only a teenager, especially the widow's walk."

"The view from up there is incredible."

"You remember the day I let you take a peek?" Mrs. Langmore's eyes grew sharp, as if all the memories had come into keen focus.

"I do. It made me realize how much bigger the world was than Walleye Point."

"Yet I spent all my years in that house." She smoothed a hand across the blanket on her lap. "My grandfather believed in leaving a legacy. He made a fortune in the steel industry. And now the Langmore name ends with me." The statement sounded more fact than regret. Mrs. Langmore seemed to have lived the life she wanted to live. She took elaborate trips, participated in philanthropic endeavors, and spent her time indulging in hobbies like gardening. Her time was her own.

Mrs. Langmore's features grew pinched. "I've had plenty of offers for the land. For the house." She shook her head, seeming distracted. "It needs a new caretaker. Someone to love it as much as I did."

My mouth went dry, knowing what I knew about the Morettis' eagerness to purchase the land to build a hotel. Would anyone be willing to spend the fortune it would take to return the home to its former glory?

"When I was young, I thought I'd marry and have children." Mrs. Langmore's reminiscing snapped me out of my reverie. "But I had a good life."

"Nothing wrong with being single," I said, eager to lighten the mood. It wasn't like I had excelled in the relationship department either.

"Nothing's wrong with the occasional handsome man, either." Again that smile. I suspected Mrs. Langmore had enjoyed her share of fun when she was younger, perhaps even butting up against more than one social norm of the time.

Naturally, Nicholas Moretti came to mind. "Do you know the Moretti family?" I asked, broaching the subject carefully.

"Ah yes, they're a longtime Walleye Point family. I went to school with Bart Moretti. Heard he died of a heart attack while in bed with his lover." Mrs. Langmore reached out and touched my arm, her eyes sparkling with the scandal of it all. "And not his wife." She tilted her head. "They say your generation is going to hell in a handbasket, but let me tell you, all that hanky-panky stuff went on in my day too. We were just better at keeping secrets."

"Except poor Mr. Moretti's?" I couldn't help but laugh at my dark humor.

"Ah, the secrets that aren't so secret." Mrs. Langmore held up her hand to stifle a yawn. "Which Moretti have you met?"

"Nicholas."

"Ah, Bart's grandson, I believe." Mrs. Langmore ran her gnarled fingers across her chin. "Has he come sniffing around my property? They've been buying up a lot of it in recent years."

I was amazed at how current Mrs. Langmore was. "Yes, exactly. They have a lakefront hotel in mind."

Mrs. Langmore let out a long breath. "Over my dead body." She paused, then laughed. "I should be careful what I wish for."

I shook my head, unsure if it would be appropriate to laugh.

"Don't look so concerned. My lawyer knows exactly what I want after I'm gone."

My cheeks burned, feeling as if I had pried into business that was none of mine. Lin would be ashamed. I cleared my throat. "I'll let you rest. Can I bring you anything next time I visit?"

Her eyes brightened again. "I need to see those photos." She hesitated a beat. "And how about something sweet? Anything."

"Of course. I'll call ahead and see what day works best." I

gently squeezed the elderly woman's hand, then slipped out of the room.

As I passed all the senior citizens waiting for their next meal, or bingo, or a visitor, I couldn't help but wonder about who they were. They had led full lives perhaps as professionals, parents, or maybe both, and now it was all behind them. How many had regrets for lives not lived? Things they should have done, but now it was too late.

What an absolutely depressing thought.

I pushed through the double doors. Fresh spring air washed over my clammy skin. My life lies ahead of me. What choices would I make while I had the advantage of youth?

I didn't want regrets. Well, any *more* regrets.

11 /
nicholas

I was thinking about grabbing dinner when the deep hum of a loud muffler drew my attention to a rusted-out vehicle turning into an open spot in front of the hardware store on Bay Street. I was surprised—and pleased—to see Elizabeth climbing out of the driver's side. I hesitated a fraction before crossing the street and heading her way. I didn't want to appear overeager, yet I couldn't resist the opportunity to casually run into her.

"Hey there!"

Elizabeth paused. "Hey, yourself."

I gestured with my chin toward the hardware store entrance. "Have a project?"

"You could say that."

"Anything I could help with?" I was searching for any reason to spend more time with her. Work was quiet, so I had the rest of the evening free.

"Not unless you have a dumpster," I said with an unmistakable edge of sarcasm. "I have to get rid of some stuff."

"Ha! I'm just your guy." I pointed back at myself with two thumbs and resisted the corny expression, "Who's got two thumbs and a dumpster. This guy." Instead I tried to sound more professional. "The construction arm of the business uses dumpsters all the time You sure you need a dumpster? The town will take quite a bit of trash from the curb."

"Yeah, I'm sure." A flash of annoyance sparked in her eyes as if she resented my questioning her.

I wasn't sure why I had. What I considered a helpful suggestion might have come across as mansplaining. My aunt Gia—she ran the restaurant—had called her brothers and nephews out on it more than once.

"Thanks anyway. I don't want to put you out." She pulled on the door handle and a buzzer echoed deep inside the hardware store.

"I'll get you one. No problem. Free of charge."

"I couldn't…"

I found myself studying her mouth. She was biting her lower lip, probably considering my offer. "I promise, it's not a big deal," I pressed. "They're just sitting there." I had resorted to all-out begging her to take one. Why did this woman seem determined to refuse me?

"Okay, if you're sure." She tilted her head. "Can you have it dropped off back near my grandmother's bungalow on the Langmore property?"

"Consider it done. Tomorrow morning?"

Elizabeth's shoulders seemed to relax a bit. "Sounds good."

"Now that we have that settled, can I take you to dinner?"

That hesitant look again. I generally didn't have to work this hard to get a pretty woman to say yes to a simple invitation for food. Maybe that was why she intrigued me. That and the fact that her grandmother was going to inherit a much sought-after property. It couldn't hurt to have an "in" when the Langmore estate came on the market.

"Let me guess, you know a great Italian place." Elizabeth flashed a smile that made my insides melt.

I glanced down the street. "There's also a sub place, and a pizza place, and—"

"Italian sounds great."

"Leave your car here. We'll walk over. Unless you still wanted to run into the hardware store."

She seemed to consider it for a moment. "No, I was going to inquire about a dumpster."

"Well, then..." I held out my hand and allowed her to go ahead of me as we walked to the restaurant. The wind whipped up and blew her long brown hair, releasing the scent of floral shampoo. Something inside me shifted. I should back out before I got too involved. I had the sense that the more I got to know Elizabeth, the more likely I'd be crushed when she left Walleye Point. Would getting close to her for a potential business deal be worth the heartache?

We crossed the street and walked down a few blocks to the restaurant. I opened the door for her, and my aunt Gia was at the hostess station. She gave Elizabeth a double take, probably because she had seen us together recently. The last girl I brought home broke up with me because she refused to move to a small town. Since then, I kept dates casual, and usually out of Walleye Point.

"Hi, Aunt Gia." I placed my hand on the small of Elizabeth's back. "Have you met Elizabeth?"

My aunt leaned heavily on the hostess stand and held out her hand. "Hi, Elizabeth. Nice to meet you."

"You, too."

Gia seemed to be intrigued by Elizabeth. "Did you grow up here? You look..." Her words trailed off and were lost in a roar of cheers from a handful of men watching a hockey game at the bar. She turned in their direction. "Looks like the Sabres scored."

I pumped my fist in the air in a lackluster show of support. As much as I wanted the hometown team to go all the way, I had developed a slight indifference to the game that had consumed my life from the time I strapped on skates at age four.

"We went to high school together," I said when the noise dimmed to a dull roar.

"Ah," my aunt said, seemingly lost in thought. "What is your last name?"

"Graham." Elizabeth smiled. "My mom Jennifer grew up here, too. Perhaps you knew her."

"Ah...I believe I may have." Gia suddenly seemed agitated and her beautiful olive skin grew pale. "It's been a while." She cleared her throat. "Have a seat wherever you'd like." She held out her hand and her warm hostess smile was back in place. "As you can see, most of our guests are at the bar, glued to the hockey game."

"Thanks." I leaned in close to Elizabeth. "Seat by the window sound good?" She nodded, her long hair tickling the back of my hand as I guided her to the row of booths over-looking the marina.

I waited for Elizabeth to sit, then slid in across from her. She picked up the menu and studied it. After a beat, she lowered her menu. I hadn't touched mine. "Do you know what you want?"

You. I shrugged. "I know the menu by heart. You had the fish fry last time. Can I recommend Gia's spaghetti and meatballs?"

Elizabeth set the plastic menu aside. "Sounds good."

I tapped my hand on the table. "Let me go put in the order. Aggie's probably on her break. It'll speed things up."

A few minutes later, I returned with a bottle of red wine and two glasses. I held it up slightly. "Wine?"

"Why not?"

I had already uncorked it, so I poured her a healthy serving.

She took a sip and then tilted the glass. "This is good."

I made a mental note to remember that she enjoyed this particular wine. It might come in handy. I wanted to convince myself it was all to gain leverage when it came to the Langmore property, but I also found myself memorizing things that were entirely unbusinesslike. Like how half her mouth curved higher than the other when she was trying not to laugh, or how she dipped her head and tucked a strand of golden-brown hair behind her ear when she was nervous—based on the pink that blossomed on her cheeks. Or how she tried to do everything she could for her sick grandmother. There was a selflessness about her that I admired. It wasn't a trait my family fostered.

Elizabeth's eyes drifted toward the bar. "How come you're not watching the game?"

I made a noncommittal sound. "I had my fill of hockey growing up."

"You got the high school team to State."

Was that a hint of approval in her tone? "I did. I'm surprised you remember."

Half her mouth quirked into a grin. *See! One side higher than the other. Oh, and that sparkle in her eyes.* She was probably debating if she should make another dig about me not remembering her, but apparently she was in the mood to play nice.

"That must have been helpful when applying to colleges," she said, apropos of nothing.

"Sure. Got a big fat scholarship to Notre Dame. My father —everyone—thought I was going to get drafted by the NHL." I took another swig of my wine. "Correction: he expected—*demanded*—that I get drafted." I shook my head. "Junior Moretti doesn't *always* get what he wants."

"What did *you* want?" Elizabeth's question stopped my spiraling thoughts.

No one had ever asked me that before. Everyone presumed I'd go pro. My dream must include playing hockey. Just like Junior's dream for me. *His father's plans.*

I ran my hand across my forehead. *What did I want?* "To make my father proud." I cleared my throat. I hadn't planned on having such a deep, personal discussion, but something about Elizabeth allowed me to let my guard down. "The NHL wasn't meant to be." I did my best to sound flippant, like I always did when it came to my hockey career. But the rock-hard ball of emotion weighed heavily in my gut. I had worked all my life, only to fall short of the brass ring. "I got injured my junior year."

Elizabeth's deep eyes studied me over her glass of red wine. "I'm sorry."

I lifted the glass and drained it. "No pity party for me. I landed on my feet." My face flushed, probably from the alcohol. *Yeah, the alcohol.* "The family business wasn't my dream, but it keeps me employed." Even if my father constantly questioned my abilities, and my brothers micromanaged me. That's why I needed to buy the Langmore estate. A huge success would throw them all off my back. And I needed to get out of my head—man, I was tired of talking about myself. "How about you? Working remotely while you're in town?"

Elizabeth folded the edge of her napkin and ran her fingers across the crease, as if considering something. "I was laid off recently." She shrugged, as if it was a badge of dishonor. "The economy, and all that."

"Oh, I'm sorry. Our construction jobs have slowed up a bit too."

"On the bright side," she added, "I'm available for my grandmother. Before I got the call that she was sick, I had already moved to Buffalo and was renting a week-to-week place and trying to figure out my next steps. It was far too expensive to stay in Boston while I figured things out."

"Boston is a great town."

My cousin Aggie appeared with two big plates of spaghetti and meatballs. "Here ya go." She smiled especially big at Elizabeth, recognition in the easy way she leaned toward her. "You're becoming a regular."

"The food is great," Elizabeth said. "Thank you." After

Aggie walked away, she tasted the sauce and said, "Oh, this *is* too good," while holding her hand over her mouth.

"I told you," I said playfully.

"That you did." She swirled the pasta on her fork.

"What brought you to Boston in the first place?" I found myself eager to know more about her.

"College. Stayed afterward." Her words were muffled around a mouthful of food. She swallowed, then lowered her hand. "Lots of opportunities, and I have friends there."

"What school did you go to?" Boston was a huge college town.

She hesitated a fraction before saying, "MIT."

I released a quick breath. "Impressive. Smart woman."

She kept her gaze averted. Twirling pasta didn't take that much concentration. She cleared her throat, finally finding her voice. "All that studying in the school library paid off. I wouldn't have been able to go without scholarships."

I pointed at her with my fork. "Which explains why we didn't cross paths in high school. I'm not sure if I ever entered the library at Walleye High."

"Ha. I knew it." Her playful tone lacked any judgment. Funny thing, I had never wanted to be considered studious. Until now.

"You going back to Boston?" I asked.

The jerk of her head and her quizzical expression said, "Didn't we just discuss my sick grandmother?"

I waved my hand casually. Honestly, I was paying attention. "I mean, once your grandmother is back on her feet."

"Depends on where I find a job. Buffalo is plan B."

"Would you ever consider staying?"

"In Walleye Point?" Oh, she was definitely amused now.

A warm flush washed over me. What was this woman doing to me? I was usually cool as ice. Heck, I was *the Italian Ice* during my hockey-playing days. That darn wine. Yes, I'd blame it on the wine. I cleared my throat and downplayed the question. "I imagine your grandma would love to have you close to home."

"I doubt that." Elizabeth laughed, but it sounded more cynical than humorous. "Once Lin's on her feet, she'll want me out of her hair."

elizabeth

I took another sip of wine and stared into the wineglass, feeling the heat of Nicholas's gaze after my unnecessary confession. *She'll want me out of her hair.*

"I can't imagine anyone would want you to leave," Nicholas said, his smile revealing perfect teeth.

"I appreciate the sentiment, but Lin and I aren't exactly close. She had never wanted...." I stopped myself mid-sentence. I turned and rested my chin on my shoulder and stared out the window. The lampposts on the dock cast glittering light on the lake. The sweet taste of wine tingled on my tongue. My head felt a little spacey. Maybe that was why I had shared things with Nicholas, things I rarely talked about. Or maybe being back in Walleye Point had simply brought it all back to the forefront of my mind. Spilling it to Nicholas—to whomever would listen—had been inevitable.

Sixteen-year-old me would have never dreamed I'd be spending time with the most popular kid in school. Which led me to wonder *why* he wanted to spend so much time with me. I wasn't the same nerdy girl I was back then, but still. I wasn't stupid. He had expressed interest in the Langmore property. Did he think I somehow held sway over its owner? That was ridiculous. Mrs. Langmore had zero plans to sell.

But the woman couldn't live forever.

"Do you have other family in Walleye Point?" Nicholas asked, snapping me out of my reverie.

I shook my head. "After my mom died, I came here to live with Lin. It was just me and her."

"I'm sorry. How old were you when your mom died?" He wiped his fingers on his cloth napkin.

"Twelve. The last thing Lin had wanted was to raise another kid." I held out one palm. "Yet there I was." I figured Nicholas could put the pieces together. This was why me and my grandmother weren't exactly buddy-*buddy*.

"You lived on the Langmore property all that time?" he asked.

The mention of the property made me pause for a beat. Again.

Don't be so suspicious of every guy. I could hear Malissa's voice in my head. I had a right to be after that jerk Brian used me for homework, all the while cheating on me. But again, I reminded myself that I did not own the property. Maybe Nicholas was just a nice guy. A nice, chatty guy.

Yeah, go with that. That might have been the wine talking.

"Elizabeth, are you okay?" Nicholas tilted his head to draw my attention to his face.

What a good-looking face he had, too. I hadn't realized I had a penchant for men with chiseled jaws and thick eyebrows, the kind of guy who wouldn't have given me the time of day in high school, unless he wanted me for something. *Oh my goodness, get over it already.*

"I'm fine," I said, before rewinding the conversation in my mind. Oh yeah, he was asking about my living situation when I first moved here. "I did live on the Langmore property. It was just me and Lin. When her husband, my step-grandfather, found out I needed a guardian, he gave her a choice, me or him." I hoisted my wineglass in a quasi-toast. "She chose me and never let me forget it." I set down my glass without taking a sip. Maybe if I cut myself off from the wine now, I'd stop running at the mouth. It was like I was outside myself looking down, shouting, "Would you shut up already?" But no, for some reason I felt compelled to share with him. "Without her, I would have ended up in foster care. Without Mrs. Langmore's generosity, we might not have had such a nice place to stay."

"That's tough. To lose your mom at such a young age."

I stared down at my hands and nodded, not trusting my voice. I wasn't looking for his pity. "I shouldn't have stayed away from Walleye for so long." I had left for college and barely looked back. If I had, I might have been able to help Lin deal with her hoarding before it got out of control.

Nicholas reached across the table and covered the tips of my fingers with his. The subtle touch sent a jolt of fire racing up my arm. *Must be the wine.* "You're doing a good thing. I'm sure she appreciates it."

"I hope so." I dragged my hand away and clutched it in my lap. "She needs me, and I have some free time on my hands." I hoped he didn't notice me blush.

Nicholas tapped his hand on the table, where mine had been only moments ago. "I'm glad too." He smiled, and my heart did a little flutter.

I went about eating the plate of spaghetti and immediately regretted it. The bite of meatball slid down my too-narrow throat. I took a sip of water and wiped my mouth with a napkin. "You weren't wrong about the food." It was delicious, even if my rioting emotions made it hard to swallow.

"I'm glad you like it." He folded his napkin and placed it on the table. "Maybe we can do this again sometime."

Nicholas Moretti likes me.

"I'd like that," I said before I had a chance to talk myself out of it. I deserved happiness, even if it was short-lived. What could a few dates hurt? Good food. Good company. I'd keep it light.

Aggie brought over dessert and we continued chatting about nothing and everything. Against my better judgment, we finished the bottle of wine too.

I felt warm and buzzy. Tonight had been a wonderful escape from the stress of losing my job followed by my grandmother's health concerns. I studied Nicholas's square jaw while he seemed to be distracted by something out in the marina.

He glanced down at his smartwatch. "It's mild out. Want to take a walk? Burn off these carbs?"

I smiled my agreement. He held out his hand, and I took it and slid out of the booth.

"You okay?" he asked, his deep voice vibrating through me.

"I'm doing great." I took a step and accidentally bumped into his broad chest with my shoulder. "Scuse me."

"You're excused." He gently wrapped my hand around the crook of his arm and pulled me closer. "I've got you."

My entire body was on fire.

Nicholas casually waved goodbye to a few of the employees, and I smiled as we walked past the hostess stand and out onto the street, grateful for the fresh air. We cut down an alley and ended up on a boardwalk that had been redone since I hung out here as a teen.

A cool breeze caressed my cheeks, sobering me up a bit. I slowed at the railing, gripping it with both hands and closing my eyes. The world kept moving. "How is it that a scent can take you right back?"

"Yeah," Nicholas said, his voice gruff. "What are you thinking about?"

It took all of my current mental capacity to consider his question when all I could do was focus on his solid hand on the small of my back. Heat radiated out from the subtle stroke of his thumb, the chills running up and down my spine…. *Oh my goodness.*

What am I thinking about? Other than how good it feels to be with you? How was it possible that I was the same nerdy high schooler who had spent more time with books than people? I cleared my throat, aware Nicholas was watching me, waiting for an answer. "I spent most of my teen years sitting on Lin's porch in this cozy glider with my nose in a book. The smell of the lake always takes me back to that." I lifted my eyes to his. I wish I could read his mind. "What about you?" I leaned into him, enjoying his warmth. "Does standing here take you back?"

"Other than college, I've lived here my entire life," he replied, shifting his gaze to the water.

I had the urge to touch his face, run my fingers across his whiskered jaw. I imagined it was soft.

Liquid courage.

"Share one memory," I coaxed him.

"Unlike a lot of people, I preferred the cold months."

I made a show of shuddering. With his arm around my waist, he pulled me in close, hip to hip, as we enjoyed the view. "Ah, hockey season," I said, amazed I could string a cohesive thought together.

"One winter it was so cold that they were able to put an ice rink here in the harbor. I set up a tournament to raise money for a kid who had cancer." A hint of pride laced his tone.

"Joey Yardly. Brain tumor." The name popped into my head. Our poor classmate had gotten sick at the end of freshman year.

"Yeah." Nicholas turned and his sincere gaze touched my heart. He glanced down at my lips, then up into my eyes.

I bit my lower lip and allowed a sliver of space between us. "Any idea how he's doing?" I held onto the railing, bracing for bad news.

"Turns out he's married and has three kids. Sends a Christmas card to my parents' house every year."

"That's wonderful." I released a quick breath. "That was a really cool thing you did." His chest was solid under my palm. "He was a quiet kid, like me. But man, he rocked that bald head and scar." Events like that were core memories for kids. "What prompted you to organize a fundraiser? If I remember correctly, you and Joey didn't travel in the same circles."

Nicholas lifted a shoulder, as if it was no big deal. "I felt bad for him. I heard the family was struggling to pay their bills. I read about someone else doing something like that, and it was my thing. Hockey." The wind picked up and a strand of hair got hooked on my lip. He took his time trailing his finger across my cheek to tuck the wayward strand behind my ear. "Why do you ask so many questions, Lizzy Graham?"

My pulse roared in my ears. "Elizabeth."

Nicholas leaned in close. "Elizabeth, can I kiss you?" His palm held my head in place, and his thumb moved smoothly…slowly…back and forth brushing the tender flesh behind my ear, sending a pool of warmth coiling low and deep. Instead of answering, I leaned up on my tiptoes and pressed my lips against his. I angled my head and the kiss deepened. My chin brushed across his whiskers.

Soft, just as I imagined.

He whispered against my lips. "I'll take that as a yes."

"Yes," I sighed.

With a hand to my lower back, he pulled me close, our bodies flush against one another. He threaded his fingers through my hair, holding me in place. He leaned in for another kiss, and this one had even more fire.

He groaned and eased his grip, creating an inch of space between us. "I can't believe I didn't remember you from high school. Because, Elizabeth Graham, you are unforgettable."

I tilted my head back and laughed, feeling his warm breath on my exposed neck. "You are such a smooth talker," I said, cupping his cheek.

He took my wrist and gently pulled it away. He trailed kisses from my cheek down to my neck. Then sighed his frustration as he seemed to struggle to break away. "I hate that you knew me as an immature teenager who thought the sun rose and set on me."

I brushed my knuckles across his whiskered jaw. "None of us are the same as we were back then. And thank goodness, right?"

13 /
elizabeth

The next morning I left the inn early, snagging one of the few local Uber drivers and arrived at my grandmother's house minutes before a large truck with a dumpster on a flatbed backed onto the property. The steady *beep, beep, beep* did nothing for the dull wine headache thumping inside my brain. If I wasn't afraid of incurring the wrath of my grandmother, I probably would have stayed at the main house and avoided having to clean up this mess. Mrs. Langmore had graciously extended an invitation, after all.

But it wasn't as simple as that.

I wouldn't be able to escape the icky inn that easily. I had hardly slept last night, but I couldn't place all the blame on the lumpy bed. Thoughts of Nicholas had also made me restless. I had no business starting up a relationship with him.

Silly girl, that's not what this is. He's just playing with you. That's what boys do. Lin's harsh words rang in my ears. Good grief, no wonder I had trust issues.

My face flushed at the memory of those kisses. What had I been thinking? Maybe it had been all that wine. I wasn't opposed to a spring fling—but with Nicholas Moretti, the most popular kid from high school? He did seem to be a different person now, but I sensed he'd crush my fragile heart all the same. From this point forward, I would keep things platonic.

Okay, decision made.

As if willing him into existence, Nicholas pulled up beside the truck and hopped out. "Morning," he said cheerily. Apparently he'd had his coffee. No one could be that happy this early in the morning, otherwise.

"Hello." I tried not to sound grumpy even though I was dreaming of a cup of my own. Darn, he looked like he took the time to shower, too. I hadn't bothered considering the task ahead of me. I ran a hand down my long ponytail and averted my gaze. His jeans—expensive, no doubt—fit him in all the right spots. And who knew an ordinary Bills T-shirt could look so good? Mentally I shook my head. *What is he doing here?* He said he'd send a guy. "I didn't realize you were coming, too."

"Gotta make sure everything's all set." He paused and gave me an exaggerated frown, not a serious one because I could see the glint in his brown eyes. "Is that a problem?"

I cleared my throat, feeling a little frantic. "No, I just don't want to take up your time."

He waved his hand dismissively. "I've got time for you." He strode to an empty space near the tree line, not far from my grandmother's house. "How about here?" he hollered over the idling engine of the huge truck.

"Looks good."

Nicholas ran around to the other side of the truck to give the driver instructions.

The deep hum of the diesel engine vibrated through my skull. *Ugh.* I glanced over my shoulder at my grandmother's house. Maybe he'd settle with the driver, then leave. *Please just leave.* Lin would be mortified if someone from a well-respected local family discovered how she lived.

I briefly closed my eyes. The thought of having a deep,

dark family secret exposed to the light of day for all of Walleye Point to see and criticize made my scalp prickle. Made me feel like a teenager again.

Guilt pinged my insides. My grandmother was obviously struggling with some issues, and I had been too absorbed with my shiny new life in Boston to notice.

I crossed my arms tightly over my chest to ward off the early morning chill. I watched as Nicholas directed the driver until the dumpster settled on a tarp with a loud metal-on-metal crash.

Oh my head.

The truck pulled forward and the driver hopped out. The two men had an exchange out of earshot. The man got back into the truck, and Nicholas gave him a mock salute. "Thanks, Pat." He turned and hustled over to me. "Shall we get to work?"

"Um…" Heat flooded my cheeks. "You don't have to. Really. I wasn't expecting that. The dumpster was very generous. Thank you." We had mentioned nothing last night about him helping.

"You're very welcome. But please, I'd like to help." Nicholas held up one finger. "Oh, hold up." He jogged over to his SUV and returned with a tray of coffees and donut holes from Tim Horton's café. "Double-double?" How'd he know I liked two creams and two sugars in my coffee?

I gave him a thin-lipped smile. I needed caffeine badly, but I also wanted him to leave. The aroma of coffee reached my nose and my spirits perked a bit, despite myself. "Thank you." I took a long sip of the coffee with its perfect mix of cream and sugar. The knot between my shoulders eased. This coffee might actually be worth having my grandmother's secret exposed.

Apparently, I was a cheap date.

"Before we go in, I need to tell you something," I said,

glancing toward the house. "My grandmother wasn't exactly neat."

Nicholas's eyes twinkled over his cup mid-sip before he lowered it. "You did request a dumpster."

"True, but—"

Nicholas shook his head. "You worry too much. Don't turn away help because I might be busy tomorrow and have no more time for you." His tone was meant to be playful, but my heart raced at the thought of not spending more time with him.

Inwardly I rolled my eyes. My emotions were all over the place and I fully blamed it on being back in this town. One minute I was rational, all the reasons hanging out with Nicholas Moretti was a bad, *bad* idea, the next I was accepting his offer to help. Not because I wanted him to clear Lin's junk but because I wanted to spend time with him.

Resigned, I tipped my head toward the bungalow. "Follow me. We have a lot of work to do."

We walked around to the front of the house that overlooked the lake. Lin's cluttered porch with its narrow path to the entrance was the first hint at what was inside.

Nicholas set the donut box down on the picnic table and planted his hands on his hips and glanced around. "Should we start here, or inside?"

I bit my bottom lip, debating and more than surprised at Nicholas's nonjudgmental tone.

"I don't think you understand." I set my coffee next to the box of donut holes. I pressed my palm to my forehead, trying to stop the throbbing. I wanted to see the project from his standpoint. Besides the porch junk, more stuff was stacked inside, clearly visible through the windows. My grandmother had a problem. A serious problem.

"There's nothing to understand. You have a job to do, and I'd like to help."

I raked my fingers through my ponytail. Tears tingled the

back of my eyes. I wasn't sure why I suddenly felt so emotional. Embarrassment? Gratitude? Relief that I wasn't alone in this mess anymore?

"Hey, hey," Nicholas said, taking my hand and drawing me close. "This is nothing. We'll get it cleaned up."

"Why would you want to help?" My hollow laugh was a feeble attempt to downplay my despair. "*I* don't want to help, but I don't have a choice."

He placed a chaste kiss on the back of my hand, its gentleness in sharp contrast to the electric jolt that it sent up my arm. "I enjoyed spending time with you last night."

"Me, too. But…you don't owe me anything."

"I like spending time with you. If you want me to beat it, just say the word." He took a step backward and raised an eyebrow.

I thought about the mountain of possessions to be sorted, cleaned, dumped. I was already tired and I hadn't even begun working for the day. "I won't chase you away."

"Good." He smiled.

Oh goodness, he had a great smile.

"Let's get to work." He popped another donut hole into his mouth. He seemed to gravitate toward the chocolate ones.

I nodded, panicky dread making me sweat. "My grandmother always liked to collect things and…um…" I let out a long breath. "It got out of control." Perhaps I was stating the obvious.

"One step at a time." He held out his hand. "Keys." I handed them over, and he picked his way to the front door through the junk stacked on the porch.

Once inside, icy dread pooled in my belly. Lin's disapproving gaze stalked me from every corner of the room. The first thing she'd do once she recovered was kill her granddaughter. This mess was no one's business, especially an outsider's.

Apparently sensing my distress, Nicholas gently touched my arm. "It's okay. You're not alone."

"Lin's a private person." I wasn't sure if this aversion to people came before or after her daughter, my mom, became a teen mom. No wonder my mom left Walleye Point. It was hard enough to raise a child alone, never mind doing it under the contemptuous eye of Linda Graham.

The hair at the back of my neck prickled. Sometimes I felt disloyal to my mom when I supported Lin. But she was all I had. I exhaled sharply again, wishing I could fast forward to having this mess and this town in the rearview mirror.

"I'm not looking to get into her business," Nicholas said. "I just wanted to help you get this place organized so your grandmother can come home to a safe, clean environment."

I nodded, taking a few minutes to find my voice. "Maybe we should start on the porch."

We went back outside. Nicholas took in the view of the lake beyond the accumulation of junk. "This is a nice spot."

"The perks of working for Mrs. Langmore." A soft breeze cooled the damp tendrils of my hair at the base of my neck. "There's a glider under all that mess. I think. It was my favorite place to read."

"The one you were thinking about last night," he said.

Again, tears threatened. I glanced away, embarrassed.

"You really were a nerd." Nicholas playfully nudged my arm with his elbow and laughed, seeming eager to lighten the mood.

I swatted his arm. "I was, and I'm proud of it. My idea of a good time was reading the Twilight books."

"Team Edward or Team Jacob?" Nicholas asked, surprising me.

I furrowed my brow, shocked. "You read the Twilight books?"

He pointed at himself with a thumb. "Me, read a book?"

"You watched the movies, then?" That didn't seem any more plausible.

"I was dating a girl who was obsessed with the Twilight series." He picked up a soft, wet cardboard box from the steps and tossed it on the lawn. "She forced me to watch the movies." He grabbed another box and launched it over the railing and it landed on top of the first one. "You still have time to read?"

"Yes. I make time." I picked up a broken umbrella and chucked it onto the growing heap.

"Maybe you could recommend a book. Get me into reading."

"Um...sure," I said, doubting he was serious.

Nicholas picked up another cardboard box, then set it down. "Let me grab a tarp for the trash. We can then drag it to the dumpster."

"We need to set aside anything that can be saved. I don't want Lin to think I came in here and threw away all her stuff." A familiar sense of unease wound its way up my spine. "I wish my grandmother was here." A frown pulled at my lips. "She needs to take ownership in cleaning up this mess. However, I'm pretty sure if she was here, she wouldn't allow us to get rid of anything."

"We'll be careful. Nothing important will be trashed," he said, reassuring me.

"Maybe not in our eyes."

"Hey," Nicholas said, drawing my gaze to his. "My joke about you being a nerd was a dumb one."

I shrugged. "No big deal." That was the least of my concerns.

Nicholas took a step closer. "Do you know how sexy intelligence is?" His deep voice rumbled through my core. *Sexy, huh?* "A trait a teenage boy is too immature to appreciate."

Heat flushed my cheeks. Smart women often intimidated adult men, too, but I didn't get that vibe from Nicholas. Not at all. In a bolt of confidence, I pressed my hand to his chest and leaned up and brushed a kiss across his cheek. "Stop with the sweet talk. We have a dumpster to fill." I gently pushed him away. "Better get to work."

"Yes, boss." Nicholas playfully saluted me.

We made short work of clearing the porch. Apparently Lin had used it as a staging area for empty packaging from her many online orders. Up until now, the decision on what to discard had been an easy one. We moved inside and worked in companionable silence, only discussing an item here or there—Keep? Toss? Eventually, I relaxed, trusting Nicholas not to discard anything questionable without first asking.

Several hours later, I found myself sitting in the only clear spot on the couch. Based on the papers surrounding me, Lin must have sorted her mail here. Recently, too.

My vision eventually grew blurry and I stood, pressing my hands into the small of my back. I let out a soft groan of frustration.

Nicholas poked his head out from behind a stack of Target bags. "Doing okay over there?"

"This is going to take forever. Maybe you could get one of those little Bobcat thingies. Does your company have those?"

"Bobcat thingies?"

Holy moly, his entire face transformed when he smiled.

"Yes, we do. Bobcats don't allow for sorting, however. We need to sort."

"There's no way my grandmother knows what's in all these piles." I scratched the top of my head, suddenly feeling anxious. This was going to take forever. "What time is it?"

Nicholas glanced at his watch. "Four."

I jerked my head back. "You're kidding me." Then my stomach grumbled. "The only thing I've eaten all day were those Timbits." I'd grab one from the box every time I walked past the picnic table.

"Me, too." He lifted an eyebrow. "Donut holes were

clutch." He reached out and took my hand and hoisted me from my nest on the couch. "Let's get some air."

I blinked rapidly, trying to focus my tired eyes.

Navigating around several tarps stacked with my grandmother's things, he led me to the picnic table. We had made more headway than I had realized. Just having the porch clear had made a huge difference. This glimmer of hope gave me a jolt of energy. Maybe I did have a few more hours of work left in me today.

"Sit." He pointed at the bench and pulled out his phone. "Feel like some burgers? Tacos? What do you want?"

"A fairy godmother to clean this house and keep it that way."

One of his eyebrows arched almost imperceptibly. "You look like you could go for a big fat cheeseburger."

I touched my hair, suddenly worried I looked as grungy as I felt. "Oh, I don't want to go out to eat."

"That's why they invented delivery."

I stretched my legs out in front of me and rolled my ankles. It felt so good after being in cramped quarters, hunched over piles, sorting things. I was done resisting Nicholas's generous offers. "That sounds awesome. Order me whatever you're having. I could eat anything." I might have prioritized a shower and a change of clothes if I wasn't so ravenous.

Nicholas ordered food and a couple of beers, then went about covering up the items we wanted to save with another tarp in case it rained. I had no idea who I thought Nicholas Moretti had been in high school, but it hadn't been this thoughtful man. I had been wrong about him.

Very wrong.

14 /
elizabeth

A short time later, I grabbed the roll of paper towels next to the kitchen sink and dried my hands. The kitchen smelled like lemons and not rotting food. We were making headway, thank goodness.

Through the small window, cloudy from grime, I saw the Uber Eats guy. He parked in front of the main house and hopped out. He glanced at the bag, then up at the old Victorian, then back at the food. Even from this distance, I could register his confusion. I was about to run out and flag him down, but apparently Nicholas had the same idea. He jogged across the lawn, gesturing to Lin's house. I suspected Nicholas was reassuring the man that it was an honest mistake and was then giving him a generous tip. That was how he rolled.

I grabbed paper plates and napkins and met Nicholas on the porch.

"Food's here." Nicholas appeared at the bottom of the steps and hoisted the grease-stained bag.

My stomach growled. "Not a moment too soon."

We sat down on the same side of the picnic table, affording us both an expansive view of the lake. We unwrapped our burgers and dug in. Apparently, he was as hungry as I was.

I swiped at a blob of ketchup on the corner of my mouth. Ordinarily I would have felt self-conscious eating this aggressively around a date, not that this was a date or anything. But everything felt easy around Nicholas. Comfortable.

"Thanks." I wiped my fingers and mouth with a napkin. "This burger is the best I've ever had." I laughed. "I was so hungry I could have eaten my shoe." I winced at the thought of actually eating my shoe. I had stepped in all sorts of gross things today.

"Glad you didn't have to resort to that." He widened his eyes and gave me an exaggerated shudder. "I was hungry, too. We probably should grab some snacks to have around while we're working next time."

"Next time?" So much for following through with my decision earlier this morning to put our relationship back on platonic footing. *Easy girl, he's only being nice.*

"Things have been a little slow around the office." He ran his palms down the thighs of his jeans. "I like to keep busy."

"I appreciate it, but this is a crummy job."

"What is it they say? Don't look a gift horse in the mouth?"

I glanced over my shoulder at the house. The glider *had* been under all those Amazon boxes. Now it sat unused and dirty on the porch. A power wash, fresh coat of paint, and new cushions, and I'd have my cozy reading nook again. I could see myself having my morning coffee out there.

Am I really thinking about staying in Walleye Point?

Only until Lin is back on her feet. Yes, only until then.

"I appreciate it," I said, not wanting to seem ungrateful. The sheer number of things that had to be taken care of—and over which I felt I had no control—made my Type A personality glitch.

No job.

No permanent address.

No timeline on Lin's recovery. *Please let her recover.*

So. Many. Things.

And definitely no fling with Nicholas Moretti.

Unless I stay in Walleye Point…why not?

From a practical standpoint, there were more reasons to stay than leave, except I loved Boston. Then again…

My gaze drifted to the old Victorian, only a section visible from my vantage point. I loved that house almost as much as its owner. Exploring the stately home had made me fall in love with the idea of studying architecture in the first place. Was the sweet woman serious about having it updated? A bubble of excitement made my belly do a little whoop-whoop. Could I do right by Mrs. Langmore's family home? A project like this would be huge for my portfolio…and I did need to find a new job.

"Hey." Nicholas touched my arm gently. "You look concerned. What are you thinking about?"

I smiled slowly, feeling the backbreaking work of the day catch up to every muscle in my body now that I was sitting down. "So many things." Things I wasn't ready to share. The Moretti family had their own vision for this land, and I didn't want to burst my bubble yet. I could imagine Nicholas trying to tell me all the reasons a personal renovation project was foolhardy. I'd need a way to make the estate self-supporting, not just improve it with shiny updates. I didn't actually know Mrs. Langmore's financial situation. If she had the money, wouldn't she have maintained the property all along?

"It's a gorgeous evening," Nicholas said, snapping me out of my spiraling thoughts. "Want to go down to the beach?" He picked up our half-full beer bottles and handed me one. The tilt of his head and his crooked smile were just as alluring as the thought of dipping my aching feet in the lake.

"Sure." That little voice in the back of my head scolded me

again. I enjoyed Nicholas's company. Perhaps a little too much.

"Come on, then."

He reached for my free hand and I realized how comfortably we walked hand in hand. I was grateful for the soft breeze as he led me to the wooden stairway that descended sharply to the beach, a good three stories below. I froze and squeezed his hand, tugging him back from the ledge. "Maybe we should pass. The steps look rickety."

Nicholas stomped on a gray, weathered plank, testing its stability. "I did a quick inspection earlier. It needs repair, maybe even replacement, but we're fine." A slight twitch of his lips suggested he wasn't one hundred percent sure. Or maybe I was projecting my own fears. "Just watch your step. We'll go slow." He guided me forward, releasing my grip and moving his hand to my waist.

The first plank groaned under my tentative step and I pulled back, slamming into his chest. His very firm chest. If I wasn't so freaked about tumbling thirty feet to the rocky beach below, I might have wondered how much he worked out to get so fit.

"Oh, I don't know about this." My stomach bottomed out, and waves of apprehension pulsed through me. My emotions were all over the place. I caught myself before my panic made me flee to the recently cleaned-off porch.

"Trust me," he whispered close to my ear. "It's not going to collapse."

I tilted my head to look up at him. His gaze seemed to peer into my soul, and my insides turned to mush. I wanted nothing more than to believe him. To trust him. But it was a skill that didn't come easily. I had already suffered so much loss.

Something in the depths of his brown eyes made me nod. "Okay."

Without looking away, Nicholas reached down. His

fingers brushed the inside of my wrist, sending shivers up my spine and clouding my judgment. "Here," he said, snapping me out of my fog and slipping the beer bottle from my hand. "I'll carry it down." He held both bottles in one hand and then found my other hand, interlacing our fingers.

The slow descent down the rickety old staircase would have had me in all-out panic mode if not for Nicholas's constant reassurances. My free hand hovered over the gray weathered wood, ready to grab it if the worst happened.

When we reached the final landing, he pulled me close and playfully bumped my shoulder with his bicep. "See, we made it."

I shuffle-stepped to the edge. It was a drop to the beach without any stairs. "I thought you inspected this."

Nicholas tucked his chin and smirked. "You're not deterred that easily, are you? We can manage—what?—a six-foot drop." Without waiting for an answer, he released my hand and jumped onto the sand, landing with a deep knee bend. The glass beer bottles clattered in his hand. He set them on a nearby rock and wiped his hand on the back of his jeans. He closed one eye and squinted up since the sun was behind me. He held out his arms. "Your turn."

I took a step back and bumped into the wood railing behind me. It gave a bit. I steadied myself and glanced down over the railing to an outcropping of rocks. *Oh, that was close.* I took a few cautious steps toward him. "You want me to jump?"

"I'll catch you." Nicholas waved his arms. "Come on."

Thankfully, this side was all sand. I shuffle-walked a few steps closer, trying to stall so I could muster up my nerve.

He laughed. "You should see your face. It's a few feet, not the Grand Canyon. Here." He turned around. "Place your hands on my shoulders and hop on. I'll give you a piggyback ride."

I was way overthinking this and I knew it. But the silly

buildup had made it even more difficult for me to get down. *Nothing is going to happen to me.* I leaned over and planted my hands on his broad shoulders. "Um…" I was wondering if I should jump onto him, or wrap one leg, then the other.

Goodness. How did I get myself into this situation?

"You're burning daylight." He gave me some side-eye.

Just do it.

I adjusted my arm around his neck and took a leap of faith. Literally. He shifted forward with the momentum and gravity. I wrapped my legs around his waist. He hooked his arms around my thighs. Respectfully, of course.

"Oof," he said.

"Um…" My face grew hot. This was a bad idea.

"I'm *teasing* you." Our cheeks were practically touching. He bent, allowing me to step down into the sand. Solid ground.

"See, easy," Nicholas said.

I tilted my head. "Until we want to go back up."

"That's a problem for later. Live in the moment."

I exhaled sharply. *Easier said than done.*

He snagged the beers and handed me one.

I shrugged and accepted it. I took a sip of the lukewarm beer, then turned my gaze to the waves softly lapping against the pebbly sand. Now that we were here, I wondered if it was warm enough to soak my tired feet in the cold lake water. "I used to find the prettiest sea glass on this beach," I said, suddenly lost in another memory. "It's almost impossible to find now."

Nicholas held up his fist. "Darn you, environmentalists."

I shook my head and laughed. Nicholas was easy company. "Yeah, I suppose it's a good thing that people don't use the lake as a dump like they used to." I stopped and drew in a deep breath, trying to stay in the moment instead of allowing my mind to race ahead, to find all the reasons why spending so much time with this man was a bad, *bad* idea.

The wisps of clouds had turned gorgeous shades of red, orange, and yellow.

He softly brushed my bare arm. "Want to sit?"

I looked over to see a boulder big enough for two. He took my hand, guiding me over the uneven rocks. He gently pulled me down next to him on the rock. The warmth radiating off his body felt good. I took another sip of beer. He did the same, then planted his bottle in the sand, twisting it a bit to make sure it stood up.

He rubbed his hands together, then leaned forward and rested his elbows on his thighs. "When you came down here as a kid, did you ever think you'd be where you are now?"

I angled my head to read his expression. "You didn't strike me as wistful."

"There's a lot about me you don't know." His pensive tone made me sit up straight.

"I didn't mean to be dismissive."

"You're fine." Nicholas bumped my shoulder with his. "Certain things remind me of growing up here."

"I know what you mean." I kept my gaze on the darkening horizon. I used to sit on the porch and read until I couldn't see the page anymore. Even then, I spent my time trying to escape this place. "And the answer is yes and no."

His mouth twitched, as if he didn't understand what I was talking about.

"You asked me if I ever thought I'd be where I am now." I ran my hands up and down the thighs of my jeans. "I always wanted to be an architect, so that tracks. But I didn't think I'd be downsized and back here." I allowed my gaze to go unfocused. A pair of gulls dipped toward the lake, then high into the evening sky. "How about you?"

"I thought hockey was going to be my life."

I turned my attention toward him, registering his stern expression. "How many youth athletes go on to play professionally anyway? The odds had to be stacked against you."

"Morettis never fail," he said, his tone even.

"Never?" A puff of air escaped my lips. Total disbelief. "Seems like high expectations."

"Didn't your grandmother have expectations?"

"Sure. She expected me to not become a teenage mom." I waggled my eyebrows at the discrepancy in expectations. "You think I'm joking but I'm not. One bad choice could derail my future."

Nicholas listened quietly, staring out over the lake.

"Once I got boobs, Lin made it clear what bad decisions she was talking about. I was told to keep my head down and study, and for goodness' sake, keep my knees together."

Nicholas turned to meet my gaze. And with one look, we burst out laughing.

"Your grandmother *did* have high expectations." He scrubbed a hand across his jaw and chuckled.

"She apparently didn't give my mother the warning enough." I twirled my wrist then held open my palm with a dramatic flair. "Ta-da! And here I am." Then I lifted my fist in mock triumph. "But I broke the streak and didn't become a teen mom, like my mother and grandmother."

"Congratulations," Nicholas said, deadpan. "Is there a medal for that?"

"Yeah, it's called opportunity."

"Well if it makes you feel better, I'm glad you're here." Nicholas sounded hesitant, as if saying as much might be too soon in this getting-to-know-you phase of our relationship.

"Me, too." *What am I doing? This man's going to break my heart. Change the subject...yes, change the subject.* "Wish my mom was still here." Whoa, not exactly the lightest of topics.

"That's tough."

He offered his sympathy, but I was somewhat numb to it. I had hardened over the past sixteen years since losing Mom. "They might have caught the cancer sooner, but we didn't have health insurance." I swiped at a gnat flying around my head.

"I'm sorry."

"Thanks," I muttered as a heaviness weighed in my chest. *Did anyone ever get over losing their mom?* It wasn't a topic I enjoyed. And it always ended the same: in awkward silence.

After a few beats, he asked, "Did your mom and grand-mother ever make peace?"

I brushed sand from the edge of the rock, fighting the swell of emotions. "Their relationship was challenging, for sure.

"My mom tried to bridge the gap a few times, but it always ended in a blowup, hard feelings, and Mom grum-bling about how awful Lin was." My cheeks burned, feeling self-conscious. "Sorry. I guess alcohol makes me chatty."

Nicholas leaned down and picked up his bottle and thumped it with his index finger. "After only one beer?"

I shrugged. "Call me a lightweight." I needed an excuse for unloading on him.

A breeze whipped up off the lake. "Being here brings back so many memories."

Nicholas smiled. "Other than college and trips here and there, I've spent my entire life here."

"Ever want to leave?" I asked, wondering what it would be like to have such deep roots.

"Kinda hard to move when you work in the family business."

"Have you considered doing something else?"

"Like what?"

"My goodness, you went to Notre Dame. I'm sure that opens doors. What did you study?"

He tapped the empty beer bottle on the side of his knee. "Drinking and partying." He cleared his throat. "Remember how I told you I got injured during my junior year?"

"Mmhmm…"

"Well, I spiraled and ended up dropping out of college."

"Tough break." I had stepped into a hornet's nest.

"Some breaks are tougher than others." He reached over and brushed a strand of hair from my face sending a flutter of butterflies swirling in my belly. "I'm doing just fine."

I felt the weight of his deflection. It was almost as if he didn't allow himself to feel his true feelings for fear of being judged. He had to be strong, successful. His father demanded it of him.

The only thing I knew about my own father was that he was gone, whatever that meant. I pulled Nicholas's hand into mine, and he squeezed it tight. "You're allowed to have your own feelings," I whispered.

Nicholas hiked a shoulder, as if to say it didn't matter, but I suspected it did. More than he'd ever admit.

15 /
nicholas

The beach was sheltered from the harshest winds, yet the shadows cast from the setting sun brought cooler temperatures to our spot on the rock. I brushed my thumb back and forth across the inside of her wrist, feeling a twinge of shame for unloading on her. She had been served up a crap sandwich more than once in her life, and she must have been fighting the urge to play the world's smallest violin for me. *Wah-wah.*

"You cold?" I asked, scooting closer to her.

"A little, but I'm not ready to go up," she whispered, seemingly lost in the moment.

I moved my arm to encircle her shoulders and tucked her close to me. She rested her head on my chest. I tried not to think about how right this felt.

By her own admission, Elizabeth Graham had no future here. And certainly not with me.

It had been seven years since I had arrived home from college without a degree or a professional hockey contract. Putting my failures behind me had been made harder by the small-town historians who took great pride in the high school team that made it all the way to the state championships. Bragging rights were gold to the long-time residents of

Walleye Point. Some had created their own version of "Whatever happened to Nicholas Moretti?" They were convinced I got drafted, had gone professional...but when pressed, couldn't recall the name of the team. Others had stopped following me when I left for South Bend. College hockey wasn't as big as, say, football, so it was easy to do. Yet others knew the truth and seemed gleeful to spread the word that the Italian Ice was back in town. Apparently a big fish in a small pond. Couldn't hack it in the big bad world.

Of course I had come back.

I had been handed a career on a silver platter, despite all the obstacles thrown in my way. My success in life had been different from what I had hoped, but it was success all the same.

A seagull swooped down and pecked at something caught between two rocks on the lakeshore, then flew away with its reward.

A slight tremble rippled through Elizabeth, who seemed to inch closer to me. I pulled her tighter and kissed the top of her head. "You *are* cold. Let's go up," I added half-heartedly.

"Hmmm, I'm comfortable," she muttered, gently patting my chest. Then she lifted her head and glanced up the steep wall. "I suppose we should. Tackling those steps in the dark doesn't sound like fun."

Reluctantly, I stood, taking both empty beer bottles and her hand. When we reached the base of the staircase that clung to the steep wall, I dropped her hand. We'd have to hoist ourselves up to the landing, a little more challenging than jumping from it.

"You ready?" I set the bottles on the platform, then laced my fingers and bent forward, creating a step for her.

She looked at my hands, and then at me. Her "are you serious" expression was cast in a beautiful glow. She glanced around as if looking for a better solution, her brown hair floating in the breeze. I wanted nothing more than to lift her up onto this landing and brush that strand of hair hooked on the corner of her mouth and—

"You sure?" Her question snapped me out of going down a road I probably shouldn't. "My shoes are dirty." She lifted her foot and squinted at the sole, confirming what she had feared.

"Come on, I don't care." Leaning forward, I motioned with my clasped hands. "We're burning daylight here." When she made no effort to use my makeshift stepstool, I said, "You can slip your shoe off if it'd make you feel better."

Elizabeth bit her lower lip. "O-kay." She dragged out the word, apparently not so sure. She toed off one sneaker, picked it up, and tossed it up onto the landing. She wobbled back and forth on her supporting leg then grabbed my shoulder in my hunched position to steady herself. She curled her pink toes hovering over the rocky sand.

"Come on..."

She placed her soft foot into my hands, and I craned my neck to look up at her. "Are you ticklish?"

Elizabeth yanked her foot back and squealed. "Don't you dare!" She clung to my T-shirt to stop from falling over.

I laughed and shook my head. "I only asked. Come on, give me your foot. I won't tickle you."

She tentatively stepped into my clasped hands, and I hoisted her up. She shifted her bum and landed on the edge, allowing her legs to dangle.

I held out my hand. "Give me your shoe."

Elizabeth leaned back and snagged it from where it had landed. I gently slipped it on her foot and laced it up. She crossed her ankles and swung her legs, seemingly uncomfortable. "How are you going to get up?" She gave me a shy smile. The light created a halo around her windswept hair.

I playfully fisted my hands and curled my arms, revealing my bicep muscles. "Me strong."

"I hope so because I'm way too tired to haul your tush up here."

"That's the thanks I get?" I waved my hands, indicating the need for more space. "Scooch over. Give me room."

She pressed against the pole and watched as I pulled myself up.

I stood and brushed my hands off and announced, "Parkour!" Remembering the episode of *The Office* where Michael, Dwight and Andy jumped from couch to counter to desk in an attempt to go viral.

"Nice," she said, getting to her feet. "Maybe tomorrow I'll put you to work rebuilding beach access."

I moved closer. She didn't budge.

Not at first.

Scarlet crawled up Elizabeth's face awash in the golden hour glow. She bit her bottom lip and ducked around me, giving me her back as she faced the lake. "What are we doing?" she whispered.

If I had been looking in the mirror, I'd have seen my face twitch. I did that when faced with news I didn't want to hear. I came up behind her, careful to give her space. "What do you mean? I thought we were having fun."

Elizabeth glanced over her shoulder. "I am, but..."

But what...?

"I don't want you to feel like I'm using you." She slowly turned around to face me. "I've been there in a relationship. I don't want you to help me with this monstrosity of a project in exchange for..." Her ears burned a bright red this time. "...for some stolen moments."

I couldn't help but smile. I lifted my hand to touch her chin, but after thinking better of it, dropped my hand. "Is that what we're doing? Having stolen moments."

"Oh, stop." Elizabeth gave me an exaggerated roll of the eyes.

"So, you're telling me there's zero chance you'll stay in

Walleye Point and if I help you clean out your grandmother's place, the only reward I'll get is having done a good deed?"

Elizabeth stared at me evenly. "Would that be enough?"

I scrunched up my face, as if giving it a lot of thought. "Can we have more stolen moments in between?"

Elizabeth tilted her head up and sighed heavily. "You're incorrigible."

I took a step closer. "Is that a yes?" I turned my ear toward her, waiting for an answer.

She planted her hand on my chest and kissed my cheek. "As long as you know what you're getting into."

I covered her hand with mine. "While I'm in all-out nice guy mode, why don't you come stay at my house?"

"Uh," Elizabeth sputtered. "I'm not comfortable doing that."

I gently squeezed her hand. "I promise it's just a friendly gesture. Unless, of course, you'd rather stay at the inn."

Elizabeth scoffed. We both knew the inn needed updates. "I'm not a fan of the inn." Elizabeth seemed to talk more when she was nervous, as if she was uncomfortable with silence. "Mrs. Langmore invited me to stay in the main house. I've been considering it."

"Oh, so you'll stay there, then?" I asked.

She shook her head. "My grandmother would kill me. She has always been adamant about keeping work-related boundaries, afraid we'd overstay our welcome here." Elizabeth glanced up the cliff, toward the old Victorian home.

"So, you're *not* staying at the main house?" I pressed.

Elizabeth exhaled, sagging her shoulders. "You are exhausting, you know?"

"I've been told."

She looked up at me and shook her head. I was beginning to care about her. Too bad she was going to leave.

16 /
elizabeth

***S**tay at Nicholas's house?*

A hot flush washed over me. Maybe leaving the door open to "stolen moments" had been a bad idea. Inwardly I cringed at the expression I had used to describe our relationship. *Stolen moments. Oh goodness. Gag.* Perhaps I had read one too many romance novels. But really, what would happen when a friendly gesture turned romantic and we had this big house all to ourselves?

I wasn't about to hop into his bed, even if he was Nicholas Moretti.

Apparently sensing my unease, he said, "I live at my family's home. We won't be alone, and there are guest bedrooms."

More than one?

Of course. The Morettis had a dang compound on the lake. "I don't know. It sounds like an imposition."

"It's not. I promise. It doesn't make sense to stay at the inn. Save a few bucks until your grandmother's place is all cleaned up and you can move home."

Home. I wouldn't exactly call this place home, but I understood what he had intended. I tugged on my collar. "I shouldn't." But the idea of not having to brush my teeth while wondering if that discoloration around the base of the faucet was really rust was appealing.

"Come on. We'll swing by the inn, and you can check out."

"Oh shoot, that's right. Lin's car is still parked outside the hardware store."

"No worries. I'll drop you back in town tomorrow morning to grab the car."

"Are you sure it's okay?" I asked.

"Most of my family members are vacationing in Florida. My aunt Gia and I are the only ones here. It would be silly for you not to crash at my house."

"Okay. Thank you. Let me lock up here first," I said.

After grabbing my things from the inn and checking out—with a little side-eye from the pimply night clerk—we drove to the Moretti compound (my name, not his), which was located along the lake at the end of a long driveway dotted with lampposts every twenty feet.

"Holy moly. This is more impressive than I ever could have imagined." Growing up here, I had heard that Nicholas lived in a huge lakefront house, but tall, well-manicured hedges blocked the view from the street. The high school rumor mill had churned with stories of epic parties while his parents were out of town.

Not that I would have first-hand knowledge.

Nicholas gave me a mischievous grin. "My crib." His tone was deadpan as he pulled up to a five-car garage and pushed a button, and the door slid open to a meticulously clean bay. He parked inside and cut the engine. "Don't judge me because I live with my parents."

"No judgment. I'd live here, too." I took in the footprint of the garage, which was easily three times that of Lin's bungalow. "I might never move out."

I slowly opened the car door, and Nicholas met me around the front and took my overnight bag. He placed his hand on the small of my back and led me inside past a red sports car and a Mercedes SUV.

The entrance from the garage led into a mudroom larger than the entire kitchen in my old Boston apartment. He set my bag down on a wooden bench that lined a wall, with coat hooks and cubbies on the other.

"My parents like everything in its place. Well, mostly my father, but my mother was the one who had to make sure I stayed in line. I'd come home from school, hang up my backpack, tuck my shoes under there, and only then could I have a snack."

"What about your brothers?"

"There's a big age gap. They were in middle and high school while I was little. We came home at different times. And my mother didn't claim responsibility for them. She was the 'evil' stepmother."

"Is your mom still around?" I hated being so direct, but he had primarily spoken of his father.

"Oh yeah, she mostly stays in Florida. She doesn't like the cold." He scratched the back of his head. "My father splits his time because of the business here."

"Nice that she can enjoy the warm weather."

"Better than riding my ass. I still have flashbacks of coming home, being told to hang up my backpack, wash my hands, unload my school folder." He tilted his head. "You probably remember those days."

I stared at the little cubby, imagining a young Nicky stuffing his *Teenage Mutant Ninja Turtles* or *Star Wars* backpack into it. I looked up at him, not wanting to think of the days when I came home from fifth grade to find my mother puking in the toilet after chemo. "What kind of backpack did you have?"

"L.L. Bean," he said. "Blue. That thing was indestructible."

I laughed, a mirthless sound. "I got my first backpack from

some discount store. Hello Kitty. The zipper broke before Christmas break." The hard corners of my library books poked through the Target bags I had to use for the rest of the year. A kindergartener fluent in reading was rare in my classroom. A kindergartener primed to be mean was not. Those skills seemed to be taught young. I shoved aside the memory as we entered the kitchen that could have been on the cover of one of those architecture magazines. "Are you hungry?" Nicholas asked.

"I'm good."

He took two bottles of water with expensive labels from the fridge and handed me one. "Come on, I'll show you to your room." He grabbed my bag from where we had left it in the mudroom.

I followed him down a hallway to a double-story foyer and up a curved staircase.

"You can stay in the bedroom at the end of the hall."

I snapped my mouth shut when I realized it was gaping open. "This house is beautiful. You grew up here?"

"Yep." Upstairs he slowed at a door near an open balcony overlooking the great room. He pushed it open with the palm of his hand. "There's a private bathroom. Towels in the closet. Make yourself at home."

He placed my bag on the upholstered bench at the end of my bed, and the bottled water on the bedside table. *He's so thoughtful.* He returned to the doorway where he casually leaned against its frame. I'd never be able to achieve his level of cool even if I tried. And I was too exhausted to try.

"This is great. Thank you." The room was impeccably decorated and homey, which kind of surprised me because the rest of the house looked more like a showroom—look but don't touch. The floral scent was more pleasant than the stale cigarette smoke embedded in every fabric at the inn.

Nicholas plucked at his shirt. "I'm going to shower and clean up. Would you like to sit out on the patio for a bit?

Unwind. Have some wine." Then he lifted his hands in a surrender gesture. "Unless you want to crash."

Despite wanting to pop out my gritty contacts and fall into the pile of pillows on the guest bed, I couldn't refuse Nicholas's offer. Sixteen-year-old me would be in disbelief. A smile pulled on the corners of my mouth. Maybe I should make a point of letting Cassie Parker know. Even though, by all accounts, Cassie was a reformed mean girl, it would still feel good to flaunt my newfound popularity.

Look at me now.

"Elizabeth?"

I blinked a few times and my right contact slid back into place. "I'm tired, but my mind won't shut off for a while. Wine on the patio sounds great." I glanced toward the ensuite bathroom. "After a long hot shower."

He levered off the doorframe, and a sly smile slanted his lips. My cheeks warmed at my unintended innuendo. "Meet you in the kitchen in about thirty minutes." He turned to walk away, sparing me further embarrassment.

"Thirty minutes!" I closed the door and carried my bag to the bathroom. I paused, horrified at my reflection in the framed mirror. There was a halo of frizz around my head. The touch of mascara I had applied this morning was smudged below my bloodshot eyes.

Goodness, I look like I just rolled out of bed. No idea why Nicholas is being so nice to me. Maybe he's bored and using me to pass the time.

Shoving the thought aside, I opened the glass shower door and turned on the water. I'd always wanted a rainfall shower but I was too busy paying back school loans for such luxuries. I held my hand under the spray waiting for it to warm to the perfect temperature.

After my luxurious shower, I threw on sweats and a sweatshirt and glasses. If I wasn't going downstairs, I would have put on my jammies. I went to the window and opened the blind. The moon glittered on the still water. If I followed the shoreline about a mile or so east, I'd find Lin's bungalow sitting on the cliff, waiting to be purged of all its belongings. It was hard to believe me and Nicholas had lived on the same lake but had very different upbringings.

My phone alarm dinged, indicating that thirty minutes had passed. I rushed back to the bathroom and ran a brush through my wet hair. I finger-raked it over one shoulder, hoping it would dry. I hated going to sleep with wet hair. Leaning close to the mirror, I pressed on the circles under my eyes. "I hope the patio is dark," I muttered, because Nicholas wouldn't be caught dead with such a homely woman.

I rolled back my shoulders and gave myself a scolding look. I wasn't going to let the million mean voices in my head ruin a relaxing night.

A relaxing night with Nicholas Moretti, of all people.

A flurry of excitement tingled in my belly as I hurried downstairs.

17 /
nicholas

I adjusted the flame on the gas fireplace insert on the outdoor table, its heat licking at my cheeks. A flick of a switch sure beat gathering wood and kindling. I looked up to find Elizabeth pulling open the glass sliding door leading to the stamped concrete patio.

"Hello," she said shyly, running her fingers through her long hair that made the shoulders of her sweatshirt dark with dampness.

"Join me," I patted the couch cushions next to me. "This throws off some nice heat. It'll feel good, especially with your wet hair."

"Great." Elizabeth scooted between the table and couch and flopped down.

I picked up the bottle of wine from the side table. I poured us both a glass and handed one to her. Elizabeth leaned back and pulled her legs up under her and cradled the glass close to her chest. The orange and red flames reflected in her eyeglasses.

"This is nice." Her voice held a dreamy quality. She pulled on an ankle, drawing her leg closer. "I needed this. Thanks." She tilted the glass, the ruby liquid glistened in the flames.

"This is really good." A slow smile brightened her face. "This is the same wine we had at the restaurant."

I cocked an eyebrow. She remembered. "You liked it."

"A man who pays attention." She took another sip.

"I try." I tilted my chin toward her. "Speaking of which, I like your glasses."

"Thanks." She touched the side of the frames. Sensing a twinge of self-consciousness, I regretted mentioning them, even though they did look cute. Maybe a little sexy.

"Can I get you something to eat?" I asked.

"Gosh, no. I'm still stuffed from those burgers." She took another sip of wine, then sighed. "I'd love to live on the water again."

"It's nice." I planted my foot and gently rocked the glider back and forth. We sat like this for a stretch until Elizabeth finished her wine and balanced the stem of the glass on her leg.

"I should go to bed. Tomorrow is going to be another long day." Elizabeth stretched out her legs and made like she was going to stand.

"Of course." I scooched forward. "I'll walk you in."

Elizabeth held up a hand. "No, I can find my way. Stay, enjoy the evening."

I nodded slowly afraid of what awkward situation I might put myself in if I followed her in. After she disappeared into the house, I leaned back and stared absentmindedly into the flames, a million thoughts swirling in my head. I wasn't going to sleep anytime soon.

Eventually I'd drifted into that hazy zone between wakefulness and sleep when I heard the slider opening. I sat up and turned, thinking maybe Elizabeth needed something. Instead, my aunt Gia had stepped out onto the patio, leaning heavily on her cane. Her limp became more pronounced when she was tired.

"Hey there. Busy night?" I asked. Even though she had plenty of help at the restaurant, she usually stayed until closing. That place was her baby.

"For sure. You know how it is the first few warm nights of the season. Everyone starts thinking of summer and eating out on the patio." Gia planted her cane, then twisted to sit down. She held her hands up to the flames and sighed. "Remember the old days when your dad would send you and your brothers to the beach to gather sticks and then scold you when they were too wet? Now you just have to replace the gas tank under the table when it runs out."

"If my brothers and I were still kids, Dad would time us to see who could change out the tank the fastest. Of course, Sal would win, Dom would pummel him, and I'd get yelled at for not hustling."

"Things were always a competition." Gia rubbed her hands together. "But that's my big brother for you. I never liked how he pitted you boys against one another."

"Was Grandpa like that?"

Gia shook her head. "Not with me. He didn't give me a chance to compete. He handed the brass ring to your father for one reason and one reason only."

"He was a man."

Gia tapped her nose with her index finger. "Why do you think I became so competitive in my own right?" She had been a top-ranked skier in high school and was expected to go to the Olympics. Until the accident.

To her credit, Gia never complained, although sometimes she winced when she didn't think anyone was watching her.

"Hey," Gia said, as if something had just popped into her head.

No, I wasn't buying it. Almost every night, she unwound with a sitcom in her bedroom without muttering much of anything to her family. Running a restaurant seemed far more grueling than managing the family business. My aunt had come out here because she had something on her mind.

"I heard someone upstairs." There was a hint of a question in her tone.

"My friend Elizabeth."

Gia stared out over the star-studded horizon. "The woman from the diner. You've been spending a lot of time together." There was a faraway quality to her voice.

"Yeah. She has a lot going on." I scrubbed a hand across my face and stifled a yawn, while debating how much I should share. The Grahams valued their privacy. "I've been helping her around her grandmother's house on the Langmore property. She needs a place to stay until it's ready."

"Look at you, being all philanthropic. Don't let your dad hear. He might think you have too much time on your hands."

"Like my brothers who are playing golf in Florida?" I snapped, not so much at my aunt but at the idea that my brothers got a free pass when it came to squeezing in eighteen rounds.

The warm glow of the fireplace caught a smile flickering on her lips. "Lots of deals made on the golf course." She sat up straight and spoke in a deep, mocking tone reminiscent of my grandfather. "It's not play. It's work."

Despite her casual tone there was a melancholy in the sudden downturn of her lips. Did she resent that her brother had inherited everything their father—my grandfather—had created, and now the next generation was reaping the rewards?

I always felt a special kinship with Gia; the two of us were outsiders. She had been forced out because of her gender, and her big chance to prove she was a winner was destroyed when her leg was mangled in a car accident. In a similar fashion, my attempts to earn my stripes had ultimately fallen short after a few early successes on the rink.

You're only as good as your last game, Dad used to say.

"Are you interested in her?" Gia asked.

I looked up at the house. "Elizabeth?"

Gia laughed.

I sighed. "She's a former classmate. A friend."

"Oh, that wasn't an answer." Crossing her arms, she leaned back in the chair, looking rather smug.

Two could play that game. "What about you? Any new prospects?" Gia had been divorced for over ten years now. She was only seventeen years older than me, and we shared a special bond, more like brother and sister.

"The only people I meet are the ones who come into my restaurant." She sighed.

I turned up my palms. "What, not good enough for you?"

"Goodness, I don't have time."

"What about one of those dating apps?" I had used them myself a few times, but usually the shine wore off after a couple of dates. And I got tired of traveling to Buffalo or Erie to meet someone.

"Pass."

A light popped on upstairs in the guest bedroom window.

My aunt noticed, too. "At least you didn't need an app to meet someone this time."

"We're just friends," I repeated.

"Who decided that?" She traced the wicker on the arm of the chair.

"She's not sticking around."

Gia wagged her finger at me playfully. "Ah, that's why you've friend-zoned her."

"Is that a thing?"

"Of course it is."

I slouched in the cushions and stared up at the sky. A thin layer of clouds floated across the moon. "To be honest, I was the one who was friend-zoned." I might have been willing to take my chances, if only she had been.

"Sounds like a smart woman."

"Can't deny that," I said.

"Maybe you should stop torturing yourself." Gia lifted a knowing eyebrow. I opened my mouth, and Gia held up her hand. "I know, I know, you're helping her out. You're only friends."

Feeling a little defensive, I blurted out, "It can't hurt to be close to someone who is friendly with Mrs. Langmore. Puts me first in line when the old lady decides to sell."

"Elizabeth has that much pull?" My aunt's tone held an air of surprise.

I shrugged. What Gia didn't know was that Linda Graham was going to inherit everything.

You are an awful person.

I shook away the thought, afraid my family's cutthroat ways pulsed through my veins too.

Or maybe it's easier to lie to myself. To claim my only interest in Elizabeth is professional because it stings that she's holding me at arm's length. Like everyone in the family—except Gia—seems to do.

"You've been a good student of the Moretti ways." Gia's words snapped me out of my reverie.

Ouch.

Gia planted her hands on the top of the cane and pushed herself to her feet. "I'm gonna hit the sack. Breakfast shift comes bright and early." At the restaurant, Gia was always the first to arrive, unlocking the doors and getting everything prepped.

Gia Moretti had been dealt some tragic blows in life, including the auto accident that changed the trajectory of her life. We rarely talked about it. I respected that. But something seemed to be on her mind tonight. Something she apparently wasn't ready to get off her chest.

Did it have to do with Elizabeth? Or her family? Or perhaps my aunt was considering her stake in the next Moretti project. The new hotel would need a restaurant.

I clicked a button, killing the flames on the gas fireplace. I reached down and twisted the valve on the tank. Once inside, I immediately went upstairs, unable to stop thinking about Elizabeth sleeping a few doors down in the guest room. Too bad I had been friend-zoned.

18 /
elizabeth

I rose with the sun, despite the mattress being the best one I'd ever slept on. Another luxury of the rich. After showering and dressing, I slipped downstairs, craving a cup of coffee.

I glanced around the spacious kitchen, hoping I could find a simple coffee maker. Instead, a fancy machine with shiny knobs and levers taunted me. Yeah, no way I'd be able to operate that.

"Took me a while to figure it out, too."

I turned to find the woman I had seen at the restaurant. Nicholas's aunt. "Hello. I hope I didn't wake you up."

"Nope, I live to wake up before the sun." She hooked her cane on the back of a stool. "I'm Nicholas's aunt Gia. We met at the restaurant."

"Yes, I remember. Good morning." I shook her hand. Hers was a solid handshake with a hint of a callus on her index finger. "The restaurant gets you up early."

"And keeps me up late." Leaning heavily on the counter, she crossed to the drawers under the fancy coffee machine. "Let me help you. Dominic will freak if someone messes with his baby." Her flippant tone suggested even she saw the equipment as an extravagance.

I was about to protest but realized if I did, I'd have to wait to get my morning fix. This "baby" looked like you'd need an engineering degree to operate it.

Gia filled the reservoir, measured the grounds, twisted that knob and pulled this lever. After some hissing and spritzing, the fancy machine produced two cups of deep, rich, aromatic coffee.

"Here ya go. We have a few kinds of creamers, half-and-half, sugar. I take mine black, so help yourself." Gia slid a cup in front of me on the granite island, and I let out a happy sigh.

"Thanks." I picked up the mug and inhaled the yummy scent of coffee. I opened the fridge and grabbed the half-and-half. After fixing my coffee to the perfect shade of tan, I searched for something to say, finally settling on, "The food is really good at your restaurant."

"Our chef is amazing." Gia took a sip of coffee, then met my gaze. "Nicholas tells me you're in town temporarily." She furrowed her brow, showing just the right amount of concern. "Your grandmother is sick."

I nodded, curious how much Nicholas had shared. "Yes, but she's recovering."

"That's good to hear. Mrs. Graham was always a tough cookie. I'm sure she'll bounce back."

I set down my coffee. "How do you know my grandmother?"

Gia stared at a spot in the center of the island. "I was friends with your mom."

"Really?" A lump of emotion made my voice go high-pitched. "You knew my mom?"

"Yeah." Gia sat down on a counter-height stool and took a long sip of coffee, suddenly seeming to grow contemplative. "We were the best of friends in middle and high school." She worked her bottom lip thoughtfully. Her deliberate manner was making me twitchy. *Tell me about my mom.* "We had a few rough patches, though." She exhaled sharply through her nose. "Girls can be rough at that age." She laughed, but it didn't ring true. It seemed as if Gia was trying to make light of their "rough patches."

"You're telling me. I moved here midway through middle school. Worst time ever." I decided to play along. Gia wasn't wrong. Girls could be rough.

"Tough time to have to move." Pink splotches bloomed on Gia's cheeks, as if the timing of things had just registered with my mom's old friend. "Was that after your mom died?"

"Yeah, I had to move in with Lin." I took a sip of coffee to mask the tremble in my voice. The liquid soured in my belly. It needed more half and half, but it could wait. "What was my mom like back then?"

Gia met my gaze. There was something very sober in those eyes. "She was on the smart track in high school." She lifted a shoulder. "I wasn't. I would have never made it through Trig without her."

"My mom helped me with math, too." My mother's intelligence was the one characteristic that made Lin proud of her only daughter. Yet, on the other hand, she'd add, *Your mother had book smarts but not a lick of common sense.*

"Jenn could have done anything." Gia pushed away from the counter and the stool screeched, but she made no further effort to stand.

"Did she play sports?" I paused a beat, realizing I sounded like I had mainlined caffeine. "My grandmother would shut me down when I asked too many questions, telling me she wouldn't speak ill of the dead. Harsh, right? I was asking about sports or interests, not for any dark secrets."

"Mrs. Graham was a tough one. Jennifer and I bonded over our super strict parents. We liked to push the limits. Neither of us played sports. We enjoyed our chill-out time too much." The shadow of a memory flickered across Gia's features. I wished I could have captured it.

"I wasn't athletic either," I said. "I studied a lot, too. Your nephew would probably call me a nerd."

"School came easy for your mom. At least, she made it look that way." Gia laughed softly. "She liked to party, too. In high school." Gia set down her mug and paused, seeming to reflect on something. "Walleye High is pretty big, but the town is small."

"Did you know my dad?" I didn't realize I was going to ask the question until it was out of my mouth. My pulse whooshed in my ears, and I couldn't believe my luck. Nicholas's aunt might just be able to unlock a long-held mystery. No one talked about him. I had been led to believe he was a bad guy who knocked up my mom and promptly disappeared. And good riddance, don't let the screen door hit you on the way out.

Gia hesitated, then straightened her frame as if she had just remembered the answer to a difficult exam question. "You don't know anything about him?" Disbelief narrowed her eyes.

I shook my head, and the world around me slowed down. This was it.

"Your father was a transplant," Gia whispered, as if she was dishonoring her friend's memory. "His family only lived here for a year. He was one of those kids who got a lot of attention because he was new in town." Gia smiled wistfully. "It didn't hurt that he was really cute." She tilted her head and studied my face. "I think you have his nose."

Without thinking, I touched the tip of my nose. A million questions bounced around my head, but I was afraid if I asked them, Gia would clam up. As it was, she seemed to be finding her own way of revealing the long-held secrets of the past. I held my breath as Gia ran her palms along the edge of the granite countertop. "I often felt bad..." Her voice trailed off and she gave her head a quick shake, as if coming out of a trance. "No sense stewing in the past."

Yes, yes, I want to stew. Please.

"All I can say is that Jennifer was determined to get out of Walleye Point. Kinda like you."

I felt like there was an accusation in there.

"You have to tell me more. What's my father's name?" The air had been sucked out of the room.

Gia pressed her lips together, as if she had to find the name somewhere deep in the recesses of her mind. "It was a long time ago. Maybe your mom and grandmother kept his name from you for a reason." Her face grew beet red. "I should get to the restaurant." Gia reached for her cane.

"Can we…" I sputtered. "I'd love to learn more about my mom." And my dad.

The soft edges of Gia's face grew hard. "Maybe. I don't know." She leaned heavily on her cane and released a long breath. "It's probably best if we leave the past in the past."

My heart thrummed in my chest.

"And about my nephew…" Gia's tone took on a determined air. "I love him—he's my nephew and all—and he comes off as a good guy, but he's a bit of a player." She sniffed. "Just a head's up for the daughter of an old friend. Save yourself the heartache."

"Oh…" I realized I had already lost my battle with playing cool. "We're just hanging out."

"He said the same."

"The same?" My voice wobbled. I wasn't sure why hearing this was jarring.

Because Nicholas had made a point of telling his aunt that he and I were only friends.

Isn't that the truth? Sure, but I was holding out hope that he secretly pined for me even though we have no future, neither one of us wanting a long-distance relationship.

"Last night on the patio, we talked about you." The room tilted and my mouth went dry. "He said he was helping you move your grandmother."

Before I had a chance to explain that Lin had no plans on moving, Gia continued, "The Morettis have been trying to get their hands on the Langmore property for ages." She smiled tightly, but there was a seriousness in her eyes that made the hair on my arms prickle to life. "Lucky for him, he has an inside track with you. His friend." The last two words felt like a one-two punch. I had no choice but to stand there with my mouth agape.

Gia stood, put her mug into the sink. "I better go open the restaurant."

Elizabeth croaked out a "bye."

Alone in the Morettis' impeccable kitchen, I replayed the conversation and wondered what in the world had just transpired.

elizabeth

I hoofed it to the hardware store to get the car before Nicholas woke up. I went to the hospital early, eager for a distraction after my unsettling conversation with Gia. Had I been fooled by yet another user? Gia seemed to think Nicholas had an ulterior motive for being so nice to me. He wanted the land.

I knew that from the beginning; she only confirmed it for me. I wanted to believe differently.

The doors to the ICU whooshed open, and my heart dropped. A frail-looking elderly man occupied Lin's bed.

Where is my grandmother?

I spun around, the rubber of my sneakers squeaking on the clean vinyl floor. Did I have the wrong room? I scanned each bed visible through the glass walls. Dots danced in my line of vision. Despite my panic, I felt like a Peeping Tom, intruding on the privacy of vulnerable patients.

Oh no, oh no, oh no. I should never have left her side. Now I'll never get to say goodbye.

I rushed to the nurses' station and planted my forearms on the counter. "Um, excuse me. Where is Linda Graham?" I would have been embarrassed by the high-pitched tone of my voice if I hadn't been nauseous with worry.

Is she dead? Please don't be dead.

Just then, my phone dinged in my back pocket. I ignored it. The nurse behind the desk entered some keystrokes on the computer. "Your name?

"Elizabeth. Elizabeth Graham. I'm her granddaughter."

Seeming satisfied, the nurse said, "She's been moved out of the ICU. She's now in room 112."

My breath whooshed out of my lungs, and my knees buckled a fraction before I steadied myself. "What does that mean? That's good, right?" She's no longer in the ICU. "My grandmother is improving?"

"Improving, yes." The nurse handed a file folder to a passing doctor but had her gaze trained on me. "No one called you?"

"I don't think so." I instinctively touched my phone in my back pocket but didn't pull it out. Maybe I had missed a call. Relief had me stretching a shaky hand to touch the nurse's arm. "Thank you."

The nurse gave me a distracted smile, then returned her attention to the monitor. "112 is in the other wing, back down the hallway."

I nodded, a knot of emotion growing thick in my throat.

I pushed the blue handicap-accessible button, and the doors swung open. I repeated the action for the second set of doors. I ran-walked to Lin's room. *112.* I grabbed the frame of the door and barged into the room.

My grandmother was sitting up in bed eating jello, or something that was jiggling. And green. Her peevish expression—the same one she gave me when I didn't do the dishes, was late coming home, looked at her funny, or did *anything* that displeased her—was so darn familiar that I nearly collapsed with relief. Angry Lin was better than Dead Lin any day of the week.

"You're awake! It's so good to see you." I planted a gentle kiss on the crown of her head. My grandmother's unwashed hair held a hint of a familiar shampoo scent, and my mind zinged back to the shower stall at the bungalow, cluttered with so much stuff. Lin was a proud woman who, despite living in squalor, managed to somehow wash her hair. I wrung my hands, suddenly overcome with emotion.

"What are you doing here?" My grandmother scrunched up her face and indignation sparked in her eyes.

"I heard you were...sick. I've been in town all week." I chose my words as carefully as a soldier picked their steps in a minefield.

"You shouldn't have done that." Lin's words came out clipped.

Ignoring the triggering dismissal, I forced a smile like the trained people pleaser that I was. "How do you feel?"

"I'm fine." Her pale skin, mussed hair, and huge bruise on her cheek would suggest otherwise. "A lot of fuss over nothing."

I sat on the edge of the bed, mindful of Lin's thin frame under the sterile white bedspread. I had wanted to bring a knit throw that used to live on the back of Lin's recliner, but it had been buried. Along with everything else.

She set down her spoon and pushed the rollaway breakfast tray a few inches. "Have you been by my house?" Lin averted her gaze, and before I had a chance to answer she added, "If I had known you were coming, I would have cleaned up. I got behind while helping Beverly move into assisted living." Strange, Lin had never referred to her employer by her first name, not to me anyway.

"It's fine," I said, not wanting to embarrass her. "Don't worry about it."

"I'm not worried. I'm just saying." Lin picked up the remote, then set it down. "I'd kill for a cup of coffee."

"I can see about getting you one." If I hadn't been watching, I might have missed the subtle shrug that suggested she doubted anyone would get her a coffee.

My grandmother's eyes narrowed and she reached over and ran her fingers over my hair. "What did you do to yourself?"

I looked down at the strands of hair in Lin's shaky hand. "I washed it before going to bed, so I pulled it back. You know how wild my hair gets."

"I liked it better blonde."

I tucked my chin, confused. "I've never—"

"You're always going to contradict me, aren't you?"

A familiar frustration tweaked my insides. My grandmother had been a tough old bat who suffered no fools and could never be wrong. All the clichés that had become so because they were true. I let it go, focusing on the positive. Lin was awake, improving. That was all that mattered.

Yeah, just wait until she comes home and sees what I've done. I would suffer serious blowback no matter what I did.

"Finished with your meal?" A man in a white uniform strolled in, touched the corner of the tray, and waited for Lin to push it toward him before taking it. Apparently he'd had his hand slapped before.

"I need something edible. This stuff is mush."

I cringed at Lin's rude comment. "I'm sure it's not that bad." I smiled meekly at the man from food service.

Lin released a puff of air. "Maybe *you'd* like it."

The young man shrugged at me, ignoring Lin's foul mood. A slight uptick of his eyebrows communicated, *I know what you're going through.*

"Yeah, my daughter finally decided to show up." Lin stiffened with indignation. "I could be dead and she'd be off running around having a good old time. Without a care in the world."

My cheeks fired hot, and my mind went blank.

"I'm sure that's not true," the man said. "She's here now, right?"

"I'm her granddaughter." I pressed a hand to my chest.

Lin blinked, then shook her head as if snapping out of a trance. "Of course, of course. This is Lizzy. My granddaughter." Lin's eyes grew red-rimmed, perhaps remembering her daughter was no longer alive.

I longed to comfort Lin with a hug, or even a squeeze of the hand, but I wasn't sure how that would go over. Swallowing back the emotion, I asked, "Do you know where I could get some decent coffee?"

"Sure," the man said, "there's a Tim Horton's in the lobby."

Of course. I had passed by it every time I came to visit. "Lin, I'll grab you a coffee. Sound good?"

"I'd appreciate that." Something about Lin's soft tone made my heart ache. My grandmother had always been larger than life, but right now she seemed small. Frail.

I hustled to the lobby, grabbed two coffees, and checked my phone before returning to Lin's room. Not a single text. Either Nicholas hadn't realized I had left his house bright and early this morning, or he didn't care.

Or maybe Gia had told him she'd blown his cover and he was rightfully ashamed for befriending me under false pretenses. This brought up flashbacks to Brian all over again. Get what they needed and drop me like it's hot.

Lin was jabbing the remote in the direction of the TV when I returned with the coffee. Lin discarded the remote and held out two hands. "Thank you."

"You're welcome." I found myself holding my breath. My entire life I never knew what kind of mood I'd find Lin in. My mother had often told me how strict Lin had been while she was growing up. Then she'd laugh and comment that it didn't do a bit of good. Jenn had been wild and pregnant before graduation despite—or maybe because of—Lin's constant reprimands.

"When am I getting out of here?" Lin asked. Her serene expression suggested she was savoring the coffee.

"You'll have to go to rehab for a bit." Tingles of nervousness raced up my spine and I braced for a verbal lashing about how Lin wasn't going to go. That she'd check herself out of the hospital if she had to. No one could make her do anything she didn't want to do.

"Ah..." Lin took another sip of coffee. Had the stroke fundamentally changed my grandmother's personality?

Ah? That was it? *Ah?* These flashes of docile Lin were unnerving.

I cleared my throat. "Do you have a preference? There are several rehab facilities that take your insurance."

"I want to go home." The vulnerability in her pale eyes was unfamiliar. And heartbreaking.

"Maybe it would be better if I had a chance to clean up the house first, before then." I studied Lin's face, waiting for a reaction.

"That's a lot of work for one person." Lin set the coffee down and smoothed a hand across the bedsheet.

"Don't worry. I've had some help." The stormy rage gathering behind Lin's eyes made me realize my mistake. My grandmother was down, but she wasn't out. She still had a lot of fight left in her.

"Help? Who? You brought someone into my house without my permission?"

"Nicholas Moretti. I..." I swallowed hard. On the surface, I appeared to be a put-together twenty-eight-year-old professional. Inside, I was a scared twelve-year-old who had lost my mom and now had to live with a woman who seemed angry at the world.

I am not that little girl anymore.

"It's not safe." I forced a steady tone even though my knees trembled. "You could trip over something."

Lin's lips twitched. She turned her steely gaze on me. "You have no business hanging out with a Moretti."

Of all the things I had expected my grandmother to say, it wasn't that. "You know him?"

She shook her head. "Not him. Gia. She ruined your mom's life."

"I've met her. She seems..." *What? Suspicious of my relationship with her nephew? Or rather, suspicious of her nephew's motives.* "How did she ruin Mom's life?" Was this paranoia or confusion wrought from Lin's stroke?

Lin's jaw moved, but no words came out.

"Are you okay?" I glanced toward the door, then back at Lin. "Should I get the nurse?"

Lin's uplifted eyes held a defiant gaze. "Did she tell you how she got that limp?"

I recoiled slightly as if bracing for a blow. "Gia?"

"Car accident." Lin turned up her nose. "Her family was convinced she would have gone to the Olympics in downhill skiing if she hadn't messed up her leg." Lin spat out the words, as if they tasted foul. "And they made your mom's life miserable."

"How was Mom involved?" I flicked a fingernail in a nervous tick I thought I had kicked.

"Your mom was in the car." A faraway look descended in Lin's eyes, as if she was recalling a nightmare that never lingered far in the shadows.

"Was my mom driving?" Was that why Lin believed the Morettis made my mom's life miserable? I searched my memory for any indication Mom had been in a life-altering car accident. Jenn had been adamant about seat belts and safe driving, but wasn't every mom?

Lin shook her head. "No. Not her." She pressed her thin lips together before speaking. "Another teen died at the scene."

"That's awful. Sounds like Mom was a victim, too." My skin grew clammy and regret made it itch. I shouldn't be having this conversation with Lin, not so soon after her stroke. "We don't have to talk about this now. You need to rest."

"Things were never the same after that night." Lin shook her head, seeming lost in thought, as if she was trapped in a nightmare. "It's not something I want to rehash." She took a deep breath and exhaled. "The Morettis are bad news. If your mother could see you now, she'd be very disappointed in you. Stay away from them."

I rocked back on my heels. The queen of guilt trips had struck again.

**20 /
elizabeth**

The hospital exit doors whooshed open, and I stepped aside to allow an elderly husband and wife to pass. The front wheels of the gentleman's walker got snagged on the doormat, and I bent over to adjust it.

"Thank you, dear," the woman said.

"No problem." I smiled. "Have a great day."

"We would be having a better day if we were headed out of this place," the husband said, clearly one who enjoyed engaging with people.

His wife playfully patted his arm. "Stop fussing. We won't be here long, dear. Now come on or we'll be late for your appointment."

The man lifted his walker up and over the smooth mat. "That's what you said last time."

I couldn't help but stare after the couple, feeling a sense of longing for what they had. In my close circle, it seemed I had witnessed more adult relationships implode than survive the test of time like this sweet couple's.

Once back inside my grandmother's car, the smell of cigarettes assaulted me. Oh goodness, I hadn't even considered how awful it would be to get Lin to stop smoking. *One more thing. Ugh.* I needed to vent. I checked the time. Maybe I could catch Malissa on her lunch break.

"Hey, girlie," Malissa answered on the second ring. "How's Lin?"

"Grumbling at me," I said, immediately feeling a twinge of guilt for badmouthing Lin.

"Sounds like she's getting back to herself."

"One would think so." I turned the key, and the engine sputtered a few times before finally turning over. The last thing I could afford was car repairs. I adjusted the rearview mirror to check behind me as I backed out of the spot. I was supposed to talk hands-free, but Lin's car was too old.

"You sound stressed."

The tapping of keystrokes floated over the line. Clearly Malissa was multitasking, and I felt a twinge of envy. What I wouldn't do to be lost in a work project with personal concerns relegated to a small space at the back of my brain.

"Of course you're stressed." Silence stretched between us for a beat. I could envision Malissa going into fix-it mode. She'd lean back in her office chair and swivel around to stare absentmindedly at the gorgeous Boston view. "Is your boyfriend still helping you clean out the house?"

"Would you stop?" *My boyfriend, yeah right.* I laughed, a high-pitched squeak that sounded false even in my own ears. Malissa wouldn't be fooled. I slowed at the stop sign and looked both ways. I pressed on the accelerator and the car jerked, then surged forward. "My grandmother's car is a piece of junk."

"Fingers crossed that it doesn't die," Malissa said. "That's one of the nice things about Boston. Public transportation." The exorbitant rents made it impossible to afford a car anyway. "Hey, what's on your mind? Tell me why you're wound so tight." Leave it to my college roommate to circle back to the conversation at hand.

I turned down a side street, taking a shortcut to the lake.

"I wanted to chat for a bit." I cleared my throat and Malissa gave me space. She was a fantastic listener. "Apparently my mom was in the same car accident that ended Nicholas's aunt's Olympic dreams when they were teenagers." I couldn't yet give voice to the fact that someone else had lost their life in that accident. It was unimaginable.

"That's some serious small-town coincidence."

A ding drew my attention to the dashboard warning lights. "Oh, darn it. The engine light came on." The car *chugged, chugged, chugged* to a stop along the curb, and my pounding heart made it impossible to hear Malissa. The car putt-putt-putted a few times before giving up the ghost. My face went hot as I turned the key. *Nothing.* The car was completely dead. I muttered a curse under my breath.

"You okay?" Malissa asked. "What's going on?"

"Car died. I think you jinxed me." I unbuckled the seatbelt and glanced around at the neat homes set back from the road. A tree with white flower blossoms had decorative eggs dangling from strings, leftover from Easter. I shifted in my seat. "At least I'm near the curb on a quiet street." I pounded the steering wheel with the side of a closed fist. "Shoot. Shoot. Shoot."

"Call a tow truck, then call me back so I know you're okay."

I didn't need this expense. Not that I had a choice. I couldn't leave Lin's car sitting on the road. As if reading my mind, Malissa made a suggestion. "Call your friend. He looks like the kind of guy who could jump your car." Her voice grew quiet. "Among other things."

"Stop with that." I smiled despite myself.

"You know me. Can't help it." Malissa chuckled, clearly entertaining herself. "Just call him. No sense paying for a tow truck if you don't have to."

"Lin thinks I'll be betraying my mom if I associate with

the Moretti family." Saying it out loud didn't make it seem any less twisted.

"When did you start caring what Lin thought?" Malissa nudged. "Come on, call him. An accident some thirty years ago has nothing to do with you. Or him."

"You're right." I didn't exactly sound convincing. "Nicholas's aunt also confirmed what I had feared: Nicholas is using me because he thinks I can convince Mrs. Langmore to sell her property to him."

"I'm sorry you're dealing with all of this." The clicking of keyboard keys sounded over the phone again. "I hate to do this to you, but I have a conference call starting in…oh darn it, three minutes ago."

"Go, go."

"I'm so sorry," Malissa said. "Keep me posted. Text me when you're home safe."

"Thanks. I will." I slid my finger across the screen, and the phone went dark.

I turned the key and the car was completely dead. *Still.*

I rolled my eyes and slammed my head back on the headrest. A car honked behind me and I waved, proud for not making an inappropriate gesture. "Go around, idiot." Realizing I couldn't sit here forever, I texted the only person I knew in Walleye Point who might be able to help me.

My thumb hovered over the send button for a beat before I mustered the confidence Malissa's encouragement always gave me. Heck, if Nicholas was using me, I could use him too.

> Hey there, my grandmother's car broke down. Any chance you could give me a lift?

> …

My heart began to sink. Was he debating how to respond? Maybe he didn't know who it was.

It's Elizabeth

Inwardly I cringed.

A second later, the phone rang.

"Of course I know it's you," he said, with a hint of humor. "Send me your location, I'll leave right now." Nicholas's deep voice washed over me, making me feel safe.

No, no, no, don't go there.

"Thanks."

"And Elizabeth, I'm glad you called."

I shared my location with him. And waited, wondering if he'd be so quick to save me if he knew my mother was the one who ruined his aunt's chances at the Olympic dream.

21 /
nicholas

I found Elizabeth sitting under the shade of an old oak tree with Easter eggs dangling in the wind. She was staring at her phone. I parked behind her grandmother's car and turned on the flashers, not that it was really necessary on the quiet side street.

She stood and swiped at the back of her jeans. I waved casually and hopped out of the car.

"Thanks. I didn't know who else to call," she said, sounding understandably frustrated.

"No worries. I just finished showing a house to a client. Apparently they didn't want *that* much of a fixer upper." I chuckled, hoping to elicit a smile. No such luck. I held out my hand for the car keys. "You got an early start today."

"Yeah," Elizabeth said, handing over the keys.

"Let me see about your ride." I jogged around the vehicle with its dull gray paint from years of sun exposure. I yanked the handle and the door opened with a high-pitched groan. I rested my forearm on the hood of the car and noticed Elizabeth's hangdog expression. "Don't sweat this. We'll get it fixed up. No worries."

"It's more than the stupid car." She rolled back on her

heels and her eyes flashed dark. "I have a lot on my mind, that's all," she added quickly, as if trying to walk it back.

"Care to share?"

She ran a hand down her long ponytail, seeming to make a mental calculation. She glanced away, then back at me. "Did you know my mom was in a car accident with Gia?"

The information caught me by surprise. "The one that ended her Olympic dreams?" That was how the Moretti family always referred to the accident—*the one to end her Olympic dreams.* As if the poor young driver's death wasn't worth our concern.

"The very same one." She threaded her bottom lip through her teeth, as if she was debating something. "I tried googling it"—she held up her phone— "but couldn't find much. Reception out here sucks."

I shrugged. "Other than learning my aunt got her limp from a car accident, I don't know much more about it. It happened before I was born. It's obviously a painful subject for her."

"I can imagine." Elizabeth crossed her arms over her chest, her cell phone clutched in her hand. "I don't understand why the mention of my hanging out with you agitated Lin so much. That accident was a long time ago."

"Maybe she's more worried about the things she can't control." I tapped the roof of the car.

Elizabeth tilted her head and a thin line creased the space above her cute nose.

"She has to wonder what you're doing at her home," I continued. "She must know she can't go home to all that—"

"She's definitely annoyed about that." Elizabeth cut me off. "But it was your last name she reacted to." If I hadn't been watching Elizabeth closely, I might have missed the soft shade of pink spreading up her cheeks. "Would it be too much to ask you to drive me to the library? They probably have the articles from the local newspaper archived. I need to find out more about this accident."

"Sure, whatever you need. I'd be happy to take you."

Elizabeth narrowed her gaze. "You swear you don't know anything more?"

"Just what I told you." I never thought much about my aunt's limp. She had always had it. However, Elizabeth's questions made me realize how self-involved I had been. Why hadn't I been more curious about the tragic accident that had changed my aunt's life? I scrubbed a hand across my face, a distant memory resurfacing. I had asked her about the limp once. I was just a little kid. My grandfather overheard the conversation and scolded me, making me feel ashamed. Why the strong reaction from my grandfather? Was there more to the accident? Or had his rage been the result of his profound disappointment that his only daughter had her hopes and dreams dashed?

The Morettis were a competitive bunch.

I sighed heavily and caught Elizabeth's eye.

"Okay," she said, as if accepting my answer.

I tapped the roof again, this time with some finality. "Let me see what's going on with this car."

Without waiting for a response, I ducked inside the musty car and jammed the key into the ignition. *Yep, dead.* I gave a buddy a quick call and made arrangements to have the car towed.

With that set, I emerged from the car and squinted up at the dark clouds gathering in the distance. "I got a tow coming."

"Oh, okay. How much? Do you know?" Elizabeth asked, tapping the edge of her cellphone to her chin, her eyes filled with worry.

"We'll figure that out later." I nodded toward my vehicle. "Come on, I'll take you wherever you need to go."

"How about the library?" Elizabeth asked.

elizabeth

Thunder rumbled in the distance as I hopped into Nicholas's vehicle. I had been so absorbed in my thoughts that I hadn't noticed the approaching black clouds. I loved a good thunderstorm advancing across the lake while cuddling on the porch under one of my aunt's crocheted blankets. But right now, I really wanted to get to the library to do some research on the car accident.

"The library, huh?" Nicholas asked, snapping me out of my reverie. He started the engine and put the vehicle in drive. "Where's that located?" He arched an eyebrow, and humor danced in his eyes.

You think you're so charming. A little voice in my head goaded me into holding onto my anger with a death grip. He was using me to gain access to the Langmore property. He thought I had a way of persuading Mrs. Langmore to sell it to him. Well, the joke was on him. I had zero sway. Mrs. Langmore would never want her land sold for redevelopment. And heck, I could play this game too. I needed a ride. *He* was giving me a ride. Not exactly the same thing, but still…

"Um, directions," Nicholas said as he accelerated slowly through the intersection.

I sighed heavily. "Oh, yeah, I saw on my Google search

that the library moved. It's now closer to the high school, which I suppose makes sense." I flicked my index finger across the screen of my device, happy to focus on a task. One thing at a time. "It's on the corner before the bus loop."

"Okayyy…" He chuckled. "Would it surprise you if I told you I don't know where the library used to be?"

"Would it offend you if I said 'yes'?" I laughed, despite myself.

"Not offended," Nicholas said deadpan as he adjusted the wipers against the big raindrops splashing on the windshield.

"I lived at the library," I muttered.

He made a sound of disbelief. "Another reason why we never hung out back then."

I released a puff of air, feigning offense. "All that studying, and I'm still hitching rides in the rain. Unemployed. And tasked with cleaning out my grandmother's house after she collected half of Target's Dollar Spot." Outside my window, all the familiar landmarks whizzed by through a watery veil. "I should have chilled out and had more fun in high school." *Ha.* Lin wouldn't have had any of that. I was not going to repeat the sins of my mom.

"Don't be so hard on yourself." Nicholas drummed his thumb on the steering wheel to a beat only he could hear. "Money's not everything." His somber tone caught me off guard.

"Says the man who has money." I pointed toward the upcoming road. "Turn here. The library is the building out front."

Nicholas made a sharp right into the parking lot. He found a spot, then shifted in his seat. "Take all the time you need. I've got some calls to make."

"You're not coming in?"

"Why start now?" He maintained a poker face for a beat before breaking character and winking. "I need to make a few calls."

I reached for the door handle, and Nicholas told me to wait. He unbuckled his seat belt and took off his black jacket. "Here. Stay dry."

"Thanks." I leaned forward and slid one arm, then the other, into the jacket, still warm from his body heat. I tried not to think about that as he adjusted the collar, his fingers brushing against the back of my neck, sending a chill racing up my spine. A nice tingling, not like the usual ever-present anxious vibe. I shifted, flipped up the hood, and stepped out into the rain.

Next best thing to a cold shower.

Once inside the library foyer, I pushed back the wet hood of Nicholas's raincoat. He was so darn considerate, making sure I didn't get drenched. Was it an act? A means to an end? Shaking off my distracting thoughts, I drew in a deep breath. The familiar smell of books always proved comforting. My escape.

Squaring my shoulders, I strode to the circulation desk. I did all the required things to prove I was an upstanding citizen before being assigned computer five against the wall.

I studied the keyboard before typing, thinking about all the hands that had been here before mine. The librarian had beamed with pride when she told me how the local newspaper had been digitized up to and including December 2019, and plans were in the works for the remaining years once the budget was approved.

Some poor intern tasked with that project was about to enter the newspaper's pandemic issues, small-town edition.

I found the database and entered a few keywords like *Moretti, Graham, fatal accident.* I scanned the results. I was both eager and terrified over what I might find. I clicked on a promising link. A newspaper article appeared with the headline: *Daughter of prominent Walleye Point businessman injured in drunk driving accident.*

It didn't take much scanning for Jennifer Graham's name to jump out.

Tate Chilton, 18, was killed in a one-vehicle accident on Shueles Road.

The walls grew close. Someone had died. I covered my mouth and kept reading.

Reports indicate the teen, whose family had recently moved to Walleye Point from Albany, was at the wheel. Injured in the accident were Jennifer Graham and Gia Moretti, both seniors at Walleye High School.

The article continued with information about an underage party at the Grahams' house where liquor had been served.

Miss Graham will likely face charges for providing alcohol to minors.

My heart roared in my ears and the room suddenly felt warm. I swallowed hard.

The articles made no mention of Lin. Perhaps she had been out of town. Maybe Lin's anger was self-directed. Maybe my grandmother regretted leaving her teenage daughter unsupervised.

So much speculation. So many unanswered questions.

I pressed my fist to my mouth. The books on the shelves pulsed in my peripheral vision. I kept reading, my eyes flying over the words.

Miss Graham is said to be at home recovering while Ms. Moretti is in critical but stable condition.

"Oh my…" I slumped back and gasped. I glanced around, thinking I had spoken too loudly, but no one appeared to be looking in my direction.

Why had this been kept secret from me? Then again, I was only twelve when my mom died of cancer. Perhaps if she had lived, she would have shared this cautionary tale.

Nicholas claimed he didn't know the details of his aunt's accident. That's why he didn't hesitate to invite me into the home that he shared with Gia. The articles suggested the accident was my mom's fault—she had provided alcohol—and maybe seeing me was too painful of a reminder of a horrible night.

I shuddered. With trembling hands, I sent the article to the printer and logged off. I paid ten cents and grabbed the print-out, folded it up, and slid it into my jacket pocket.

I flipped up the hood and drew in a deep breath. It smelled of Nicholas. His clean scent. Such a shame. If their backstories hadn't been riddled with so many obstacles, I might have been able to let my guard down. But it wasn't meant to be. Besides being concerned about his true motivations, I refused to be the object of his family's side-eye. Jennifer Graham had been a bad influence. She hosted an underage drinking party that killed a young man and ruined Gia Moretti's life. My mother was so much more than this awful, *awful* lapse in judgment. I would not allow myself to be surrounded by those who thought otherwise.

I would have to clear my mind long enough to deal with Nicholas and collect my things from the Morettis.' I couldn't stay there. Gia probably hated me. Maybe hate was a strong word. But the woman was quick to suggest Nicholas' interest in me was strictly for business purposes, as if she wanted to hurt me.

The striking thought gave me pause. Had Gia made the suggestion to hurt me? *Hmm...didn't I think the same thing about Nicholas's intentions?* I needed time to think.

I squared my shoulders and drew in a deep breath. I strolled through the theft detection scanners—as if library users were the thieving kind—and froze at the front doors. The gray sky, the rain splashing in the puddles, and the brisk wind suited my mood.

There were reasons I stayed away from Walleye Point. I had just uncovered a few more.

"Did you find what you were looking for?" Nicholas

asked when I slammed the passenger door, shutting out the driving rain. He was annoyingly chipper.

"Apparently, my mom hosted a party the night of the accident. They were all drinking." Mesmerized by a little girl and her mom across the parking lot, holding hands and laughing as they unsuccessfully tried to beat the rain to their minivan, I pushed the wet hood off and sighed.

"That's tough." His deep voice sounded close, as if he expected me to turn around to face him. I did, then lowered my eyes to a few coins in the cup holder in the console.

"Yep, it was. So senseless." I lifted my gaze to meet his, my cheeks burned. I couldn't talk about this. Not now. "Any update on my car?"

Nicholas shook his head. "No. My guy at the garage will call you. I gave him your cell."

"Thanks." I cleared my throat. "Would you mind taking me back to your house so I can collect my things?"

"I don't understand. We have plenty of room."

"I've decided to take Mrs. Langmore up on her offer to stay in the main house." I forced a smile, even though the weight of the world bore down on my shoulders. "I figure it'll be a good chance for me to check out the architecture and the history. I'm a geek for all that stuff. I, um, was reluctant to stay there before because Lin had always stressed that Mrs. Langmore was her boss." I tilted my head. "But Mrs. Langmore insisted."

"Uh, sure," Nicholas said. I had a hard time reading his tone. "Whatever you want."

nicholas

Standing in my family's home, I gazed across the lake while upstairs Elizabeth packed her belongings. The storm clouds hung low and dark over the murky waters. I mulled over everything Elizabeth had shared with me. I sensed she wanted nothing to do with me or any of the Morettis because of a tragic accident that happened before either of us was even born.

And I wasn't sure if I'd ever be able to fix that.

And I wanted to.

Out of sorts, I wandered over to Dom's fancy coffee maker. Maybe Elizabeth would agree to sit down and have a cup with me. She had to realize I wanted to get to know her for *her*. Spend more time with the quiet, shy girl I hadn't been smart enough to appreciate as a teen. The heck with the Langmore property.

As I crossed to the sink to fill the reservoir, I had to step over my raincoat. It must have slipped off the back of a chair. When I picked it up, a piece of paper poking out of the pocket caught my attention. I pulled it out and set it on the island. Elizabeth had obviously printed out something at the library. Probably an article about the accident.

I was distracted making coffee when a deep voice startled me. "When are we going to get a dang coffee maker I can use?"

I slowly turned around and smiled at my father's unexpected appearance. "As soon as Dom moves out."

My father exhaled sharply through his nose. "So, when hell freezes over." Junior drummed his beefy fingers on the granite island.

"Welcome home." I checked to make sure nothing was going to hiss or overflow on the fancy machine before turning my full attention to my father. "How was Florida?"

"Hot," my father said flatly. If it wasn't for my mother's insistence, he probably would have skipped the Florida trips altogether. "Couldn't stand it anymore. Caught a flight home alone this morning."

My father tapped the folded paper in a mindless gesture and continued giving me the rundown. "Dom and Diane plan to go to St. Augustine for a few days. She's got a new lease on life after all the terrible business last year. They're talking about trying for a family."

If I hadn't been studying my father's face, I might have missed the twitch of his nose.

"Sal's coming back next week." Junior unfolded the piece of paper in front of him, and I wished I had left it tucked away in the pocket of the raincoat. "They figure next year they'll be hamstrung by the kids' school schedules..." His voice trailed off as his eyes scanned the paper.

I didn't dare take the paper out of his hand or tell him it was none of his business. That wasn't how any of the Moretti sons talked to our father.

Finally he looked up, a deep vertical line carved between his busy eyebrows. "What is this?"

"I—"

"It's mine." Elizabeth set down her overnight bag on the stool and held out her hand.

If she had expected Junior to give it to her, she was sadly mistaken.

24 /
elizabeth

I lifted my chin, feigning a confidence I didn't feel. "I'll need that, please." The fire in the man's eyes made it very clear he wasn't going to hand over the paper without a fight.

Nicholas held out his arm in an introduction. "Dad, this is Elizabeth Graham."

"Yeah, I can see that. You're the spitting image of your mother." The man made no effort to offer his hand. He took a step closer and held up the paper. "Does Gia know you're here?"

"They've met," Nicholas answered for me, and I didn't know if I should be offended or thankful. But at that moment, I couldn't think straight with all the adrenaline flooding my system.

Ignoring his son, Junior Moretti shook the paper at me again. "Why do you have this?"

Nicholas opened his mouth, and I held up my hand to quiet him. The need to defend my mother—my beautiful, loving mother—swept over me. I quickly sifted through all the possible things I could say to Mr. Moretti and settled on the most direct option. "I did some research at the library about the accident my mother and your sister were in. I printed out an article."

"Why would you do that?" The man's anger seemed to be disproportionate to the perceived offense.

"Why not?" I tipped my chin toward the paper. "It's an article."

That simple question seemed to fluster the man who undoubtedly considered himself unflappable. Some sort of calculation was going on behind his steely gaze. He took a step closer and Nicholas intervened. "Father, stop. She's trying to find out more about her mom. That's all."

Junior turned his ire on his son. "How much do you know about her? She could be digging up dirt to use against our family. Don't be such a naïve ass."

I blinked back my surprise. My iron spine dissolved under his fiery gaze. I snatched my bag from the chair, knocking it over. The crash of wood on the expensive tile jarred my frayed nerves. I squared my shoulders, swallowing an apology. "I'm going."

"Wait," Nicholas said, "I'll give you a ride."

"Thanks." I turned to leave, then swung back around, my bag slamming into my hip. "I don't want anything from your family, and I'm sorry if I upset you."

The older man leaned back on his heels, apparently not used to anyone speaking to him in this manner. "You must imagine how devastating that accident was to Gia. To our entire family. And, I suppose, your mother." He added the last bit as an afterthought. If he was going for sympathy, he had failed.

All talk had been about Gia. Poor Gia. I fought my emotions. "I wouldn't know. It wasn't something my mom talked about." I was very aware of my steely tone, and I didn't care. From my perspective, my mother had made a horrible mistake as a teenager and had to live with the guilt for the rest of her life. The Moretti family certainly hadn't given her a pass.

"Hmm." Mr. Moretti shook his head and sighed, affecting an air of despair that didn't seem genuine. "I was sorry to hear your mother passed."

"Thank you," I said through a clenched jaw. I looked over at Nicholas. "Can we go?"

"Where is home nowadays?" his father asked.

"I'm staying on the Langmore property." I didn't want to share extraneous information, but I suspected he already knew plenty about me.

"Sprucing it up to get top dollar?" Mr. Moretti asked.

"It's not for sale," I stated matter-of-factly while searching his face.

Junior made an "I'm not so sure about that" sound with his lips. "She is a tough nut. I haven't been able to reach her directly in weeks. The new place stopped transferring my calls."

"You're not harassing Mrs. Langmore at the nursing home, are you?" Nicholas asked, the disgust evident in his tone.

Junior jerked his head back, creating a triple chin effect. "Harassing?" He scoffed. "The property isn't going to fall into our lap."

A muscle ticked in Nicholas's jaw. He seemed to be having an internal debate with himself. He slowly blinked, then turned and held out his hand. "Let's go."

"Wait..." I sighed heavily. "Mrs. Langmore loves her home. It would crush her to think it would all be gone after she passes."

"It would cost a fortune to maintain that old house," Junior said, seeming to mellow. "If we don't buy and tear it down, someone else will. Or it will fall apart with time." He sat down on a stool, resting his elbows on the island and tapping the pads of his fingers together. "It'll be worth nothing if no one buys the property. I have money and resources, and I'm willing to take a chance on Walleye Point." The finality in his statement suggested he considered this a done deal.

I understood Nicholas's father had a point, but I didn't want to drive down the road and see a generic hotel in its place. *You won't be living here.* But Lin would be. Where would she stay? "All I ask is that you let Mrs. Langmore live out her final days in peace." A mix of resignation and disappointment weighed on me. I turned and headed through the mudroom into the garage.

"I'm sorry about that." Nicholas opened the passenger door and I climbed in without saying a word.

When we arrived at the Langmore estate, I thanked him for the ride. I opened the door and twisted to look at him. "If I had known about the animosity between our families, I would have never—"

"Hung out with me?" Nicholas asked, studying me with those darn puppy dog eyes.

"Yeah. I didn't mean to cause you any problems with your family." I pushed the passenger door wider to climb out. "We should probably call it a day." I hesitated a beat then added, "Please, don't bother Mrs. Langmore. She's a sweet lady."

The crestfallen expression on Nicholas's face broke my heart. Despite my best efforts, this man was getting to me. "Don't judge me by my father." He ran a hand across his whiskered jaw. "I'm glad I didn't know there was some big dark secret between our families. I would have missed out on getting to know you."

"I appreciated all your help with Lin's place," I muttered, unable to hide the tremble.

"Of course." He reached out and captured my hand. The warmth of his touch sent a wave of attraction shooting up my arm. "And I didn't do it with an ulterior motive." *The Langmore house.* "Do you believe me?"

"I guess time will tell." The words flew out of my mouth before I could overthink it. I'd been burned too many times before. "Goodbye, Nicholas."

"Bye." The single word followed me out of his car. I didn't turn around to look at him. I didn't trust myself.

Do I trust him?

I had to stop by the bungalow to grab the keys to the main house. I found my grandmother's car parked along the side. Nicholas's repair guy must have dropped it off. I plucked a note out from under the windshield wiper.

> *Replaced the starter. Should be good to go.*
> *-Mike*
> *P.S. Nicky Moretti is a good guy. He pulled all sorts of favors for this one.*

I pressed the heel of my hand to my forehead as a whirlwind of emotions swept over me. Why did that jerk have to be such a nice guy?

25 /
elizabeth

Over the next couple of weeks, I finished cleaning out Lin's bedroom, bathroom, and kitchen. Well, as much as I could. After a lot of tossing, organizing, and scrubbing, there was enough space for Lin to navigate her home safely once she was released from the rehab facility. Out of respect, I took care to save many of my grandmother's "prized" possessions which were now stacked neatly along a back wall in the living room or in the spare bedroom closet.

And "good guy" Nicky Moretti seemed to respect my wish for space because he responded to my request to pick up the dumpster with businesslike efficiency.

With Lin's living situation sorted, I shifted my attention to exploring every nook and cranny of Mrs. Langmore's Victorian home. It was more incredible than I had remembered. Hundred-year-old newspapers, vintage toys, yellowing photographs, and first edition books had been forgotten in the third-floor attic. Gorgeous antiques adorned every room. Intricate moldings, antique light fixtures, hardwood floors, and stained glass windows were exactly my jam.

One of my many ideas had been to do a series called "Before and After" where I'd post improvements made to the old home. However, now I was leaning toward something like "Echoes of the Past." As a test run, I had posted some of the best images on my social media sites and people responded positively. All the hearts and likes gave me a dopamine rush.

Mrs. Langmore was tickled by the project and poured over the tiniest details as she studied the images I had loaded onto a digital frame and presented as a gift for her new residence. Mrs. Langmore spoke dreamily of my bringing her home back to life—an idea that sent an excited thrill up my spine. But that would take time and money. Mrs. Langmore had little of one, and lots of the other, but I feared I might not be able to finish the project before it was time to leave Walleye Point. And Mrs. Langmore might need her money to pay for long-term care. It didn't come cheap.

After some of the posts went viral, sponsors began to reach out to me offering me actual money for content. The hit of adrenaline each time I opened my social media apps was addicting. I went into it thinking it would be a fun hobby, getting me through until I landed my next "real" job.

The work of sorting and posting was exciting and satisfying. The days flew by and I (almost) never thought of Nicholas. *That's a lie.* Life's experience warned me I couldn't trust men, and that was only reinforced when Mrs. Langmore was informed by the front desk of repeated calls by the Morettis regarding the purchase of her property.

Nicholas claimed he wasn't using me to gain favor with Mrs. Langmore. Was he lying or was I jumping to conclusions?

Either way, why wouldn't they allow the woman to live in peace? *Ugh.*

On the morning Lin was to be released from the rehab center, I enjoyed my coffee on the porch of Lin's bungalow as I had become accustomed to doing. I had given the cushions of the glider a good scrub, and although faded from the sun, they looked clean and inviting. The sky was a brilliant blue, and the Buffalo skyline was clearly visible looking east across the lake. Spring had arrived in full force. I drew in a deep breath and released it. My sense of accomplishment was dulled by an underlying dread. How would Lin respond to learning that I had tossed a lot of her things? In my eyes, it was all garbage, but Lin's hoarding tendencies would undoubtedly cloud her judgment.

I took a long sip of coffee and gently pushed back and forth on the glider with the toe of my sneaker. Before I had a chance to lose myself in ruminations, the cell phone buzzed on the seat cushion beside me. Mrs. Langmore's number popped up. The sweet woman wanted me to come by after picking up Lin. We didn't talk long because Mrs. Langmore seemed distracted. "I'll have reception call your room when we arrive," I said, knowing Mrs. Langmore screened her visitors.

Thank you, Moretti family.

"Sounds good, dear. See you whenever you get here." She coughed softly. "Oh, if Lin is too tired, I understand, but I'd really like to see you both."

I ended the call and checked the time. I had a meeting with Lin's social worker and the rehab team in an hour about her discharge. My phone buzzed again and I smiled when my best friend's name popped up on the caller ID.

"Hi, Malissa." The familiar backdrop of windows overlooking an adjacent high-rise building in downtown Boston framed Malissa's long blond hair.

"Hey there!" She squinted into the screen. "Oh, did I catch you at a bad time?"

"Nope." I turned the phone around to display part of the porch and the lake view.

"Nice. Looks like you've made lots of progress."

"Lin comes home today." I bit my bottom lip, that familiar twinge of anxiety swirling in my gut, not a good mix with coffee. I set the mug down on the glass table next to the glider.

"Oh, perfect timing then," Malissa said, speaking fast with excitement.

"What do you mean?"

"Hey, I don't have much time. I have a meeting at nine, but we need to talk," Malissa said, not answering her question.

I studied her face. "You okay?"

"Everything is great. Sorry, I didn't mean to scare you." Malissa turned to look at something else, probably her desktop monitor. "Remember Gerry, one of my co-workers?" she whispered even though she had a private office. "That dude who thought he was the best thing since sliced bread? Don't get me wrong, he's a great architect, technically proficient, but he's about as inspiring as a deflated balloon. They axed him after one of our biggest clients complained. Anyway..." Malissa's eyes grew round, as if she was getting ready to deliver fantastic news. "My boss asked me for a referral...and of course, I gave them your name. You have your business profile updated online, right?" Malissa spoke like she had downed a double shot of espresso. I had experienced caffeine-fueled Malissa plenty during our all-nighters in college. "You've got a real shot at this job. I mean, I think it'll be yours if you want it."

My mind whirled. My profile was updated like any good unemployed college grad, but I hadn't been obsessing over it. I had been having too much fun taking photos of Mrs. Langmore's property, posting them to social media, and drafting architectural plans for updates that I would probably never do myself. The freedom to be creative on my own terms was intoxicating.

I cleared my throat. "Wow...that's great." Riding the T, answering to a demanding boss, working late nights, high rent...all flashed in my mind.

Malissa scrunched up her face. "Is it? You sound conflicted."

I smoothed the frizzy hair around the crown of my head visible in the tiny image in the lower right corner of the screen. "I guess I'm distracted. I hadn't thought an opportunity would pop up so soon in Boston." I loved Boston. The architecturally significant buildings dating back to the early days of our country, the winding cobblestone roads, the historic harbor. "I really appreciate you putting in a good word for me. I imagine they'll be bringing people in for interviews soon?"

"Next week. They're willing to interview you via Zoom." Malissa glanced away from the phone as if something had caught her attention. "Give it some thought. We can chat later, okay? I have a meeting." Her mouth twisted in an apologetic manner.

"Go, go," I said. "And Malissa, thank you so much."

"Of cours—" the call ended abruptly, as if she had pressed the end button a second too soon.

I tossed the phone on the cushion and ignored my cooling coffee on the side table. "Wow…a job in Boston," I whispered to no one, staring blankly at the lake I loved so much.

Lin was on the mend. Her home was clean. I could head back to Boston. With a job. Resume my life.

So why did my belly flutter with anxiety?

Hadn't this been my plan all along?

elizabeth

I slipped my hand around the crook of Lin's arm as we walked up the pathway to Oakwood Assisted Living, where Mrs. Langmore lived.

"Are you sure Mrs. Langmore wants us to come by today? I bring her the mail on Thursdays." Lin was a stickler for rules and never wanted to cross the line between employer and employee. Boy, my grandmother wouldn't have liked me sorting through the Langmore family's heirlooms.

But that was a problem for another day. Well, maybe today. But later.

I opened the door for my grandmother who seemed understandably slower than before the stroke. "How are you?" I asked.

Not one to be fussed over, Lin flicked her fingers dismissively. "Fine. Fine."

The receptionist looked up and smiled. "Go ahead to Mrs. Langmore's room. She's expecting you."

I led Lin down the long corridor to Mrs. Langmore's one-bedroom suite. I lifted my hand to knock and froze, hearing a familiar male voice coming from inside. Swallowing the bile rising in my throat, I twisted the doorknob. The door swung open to reveal Mrs. Langmore and

Nicholas Moretti sitting at a small table in the kitchenette area.

Forgetting Lin was standing next to me, I planted my fist on my hip. "What are you doing here? Mrs. Langmore doesn't like to be bothered with this." I pointed my open palm at the pile of official-looking papers on the table. Some nerve!

Mrs. Langmore looked up, her blue eyes soft and welcoming. I tilted my head and glanced at Nicholas, whose arched eyebrows seemed to be seeking understanding. Then, I returned my gaze to Mrs. Langmore, trying to piece together what exactly was going on here. Had Nicholas charmed her somehow? Mrs. Langmore was up in years, but she was of sound mind. Surely she wouldn't allow the Morettis to tear down her beautiful home, the one I was falling in love with all over again. A visceral sensation of resistance pulsed through me. *I* would not allow this.

Mrs. Langmore pushed slowly to her feet and crossed to Lin, giving her a warm one-arm hug. For her part, Lin stood awkwardly, her arms down by her sides. "How are you feeling?" The older woman took a step back. "You look like you could stand to gain a few pounds and get a little sun on your cheeks, but other than that..."

"I'm fine. I'll be ready to get back to work—"

"Hush," Mrs. Langmore said, not unkindly. "We'll discuss that in a minute."

What little color Lin had drained from her face. Perhaps the very real fear of losing her job had hit home now that her employer was in assisted living.

My penetrating gaze drifted to Nicholas, trying to telegraph my anger. *I can't believe you had the nerve to come here.* He stared back at me, warmth and kindness in his brown eyes. I didn't need him to pity Lin. Pity me. I wanted to say as much, but any words I had for him got trapped in my throat.

"Nicholas, would you mind giving us a few minutes? I'd

like to talk to Elizabeth and Linda." Mrs. Langmore gestured toward the door with her open palm. "You'll find comfortable couches in the sitting room." Mrs. Langmore may have been elderly, but she still had an authoritarian air about her.

Nicholas gathered up his papers. "Of course." He brushed past me with a quick nod and an apologetic look on his handsome face.

Once the door closed quietly behind him, I spun around, feeling more anger than I should have. Towards Nicholas. Towards the cruelty of time. Mrs. Langmore should still be at home, where she had lived her entire life. Getting old was tough, but having had a mother die young, I understood it was a privilege denied to many.

I glanced toward the door with the tremendous urge to do something. "Do you want me to ask reception to get rid of him?" I didn't understand how he had gotten through in the first place. Did he charm the bored receptionist?

Mrs. Langmore smiled, a knowing look in her eyes. "Dear, have a seat. Both of you. I need to share something with you."

I guided Lin to the kitchen chair, and Mrs. Langmore sat on the high-backed couch with cherrywood arms. A small antique table with an ornate knob on a partially opened drawer sat in the perfect spot in the corner. The personal furniture touches made the room cozy.

Mrs. Langmore fluttered her fingers at the end table. "Grab the papers in there and hand them to your grandmother. It's high time I've shared something. With both of you."

I slid the papers out of the drawer. I recognized the name of a local law firm on the first page. I set the papers on the table in front of my grandmother.

Lin frowned down at them; deep lines bracketed her mouth. "I don't have my glasses."

Mrs. Langmore held out her hand and waved, seemingly

growing impatient with excitement. "Elizabeth, do you have your contact things in?"

I laughed. "If I didn't have my contacts in, I wouldn't be able to see you."

"That's good news, then. Read those papers. Out loud."

I sat down on a footstool and slid the papers from the table. I read the legal-sounding jargon, then got to the crux of the documents, my heartbeat thundering loudly in my ears. With shaky hands, I lowered the papers. "You're leaving the estate to my grandmother?"

Lin gasped, clutching her chest. "Oh…"

Mrs. Langmore seemed to straighten, folding her hands on her lap, a pleased expression on her face. The walls pulsed with expectation as I tried to process all of this. Lin was going to inherit the entire Langmore estate.

"You okay, Lin?" I asked.

Lin stood on shaky legs and batted me away when I stood to help her. "No, no, no," she muttered, pivoting toward the door, then back to Mrs. Langmore, looking like a cornered cat afraid of getting her claws clipped. "I'm your employee."

"I have never married," Mrs. Langmore said in a calm, determined voice. "I have no children." In Mrs. Langmore's youth, one generally preceded the other or was met with great shame. "You've become my family, Linda, and my decision is final."

"Wow," I whispered, sitting back down. I couldn't help myself. The land alone was worth a fortune. *The land the Morettis want for their hotel.* I pushed the thought aside. Now, it seemed, the decision was Lin's. My grandmother could sell and take the money and retire. Move to Florida. Wherever she wanted.

"I can't." Lin turned and sat back down at the table, resting her hands in her lap. Her posture reminded me of a schoolgirl who had been scolded.

"The reason I didn't tell you sooner was because I knew

you'd react this way." Mrs. Langmore leaned forward, closer to her long-time employee. "We're both getting a little long in the tooth for big surprises." Her quiet laugh was inviting. "And since there seems to be some interest in the property, now is the time to make some decisions."

I bit my tongue, my mind swirling.

"The Moretti family has an interest in building a hotel on the property," Mrs. Langmore continued.

"You wouldn't sell to that awful family," Lin said, her voice cracking. "They ruined my Jennifer's life."

"I know how you feel about the Morettis, Lin." Apparently my grandmother had shared more with Mrs. Langmore than she had with me. "We need to compartmentalize things. Consider what's best. Nicholas Moretti offered a lot of money for my home." If I hadn't been watching Mrs. Langmore, I might have missed the glittering sheen in her eyes.

"You can't sell…" Lin whispered.

Mrs. Langmore sighed. "I won't have pockets in my shroud." A morbid image flashed in my mind. "Nicholas was here today—at my invitation—with an interesting proposal. The next generation of Morettis might have more ethics than those who came before them."

I swallowed hard. "Are you sure? All the Morettis are a competitive bunch."

Mrs. Langmore smiled. "Ah, he likes you, too."

I cocked my head in confusion, not trusting my voice. "I didn't say anything about liking him." My response might have come off as a little too indignant, causing fiery embarrassment to lick my cheeks.

Mrs. Langmore winked. "I could read him as well as I can read you now."

"I don't trust…" Lin said. Her dislike of the Morettis ran deep.

"You came by your feelings honestly," Mrs. Langmore said. "But Nicholas is not his aunt or grandfather. He's his own man. He was the one who let me know that my lawyer had broken confidentiality and told the Morettis that I planned to leave everything to Linda."

"Nicholas knew?" My heart dropped. *He knew.* Oddly, for someone I had already written off, that revelation stung. A lot. It only served to prove my point. And it was worse than I had initially thought. He'd used me to ingratiate himself with not Mrs. Langmore, but my own grandmother. "That's why he was trying to get close to me." I ground my teeth. *What a jerk.*

"Dear, he did me a favor," Mrs. Langmore said. "He confirmed what I suspected. I never liked that young whippersnapper at the law office. He took over his father's practice and runs it like it's his personal piggy bank. I've already obtained alternate representation."

"Nicholas was being manipulative…" I fisted my hands in my lap.

Mrs. Langmore shook her head. "I believe his intentions were pure." She smiled softly. "Don't be so quick to judge. I think we should hear out his proposal. Lin, the money allows you to travel. Do whatever you want."

"It's your family home." Lin ran a shaky hand down her hair, flattened on one side, perhaps from lying down before I had picked her up from the rehab center this morning. "I couldn't. I just couldn't."

I stood and placed a hand on my grandmother's shoulder, fully expecting her to shrug it away. She didn't. This was a huge deal. A very huge deal.

"Yes, you can and you will," Mrs. Langmore said. "Nicholas has a reasonable plan for my family home." She gestured at me. "Go fetch your friend. He can tell us all about it."

nicholas

I sat in a heavily decorated TV room next to the Oakwood Assisted Living entrance, wondering how the conversation was going in Mrs. Langmore's apartment. I wished I could have been there to see the look on their faces —especially Elizabeth's—when Mrs. Langmore revealed she was leaving her estate to Linda Graham. From what I had gleaned from Elizabeth, I'd guess that Lin would be resistant to the idea. But in the end, how could she refuse?

And what about my plan? Would Elizabeth ever forgive me for my persistence in acquiring the property? I rubbed the back of my neck, wishing the Moretti blood didn't run so deep. I hoped this new plan would prove I could be a successful businessman minus the callousness and winner-take-all ruthlessness often displayed by my father and brothers.

A soft, hesitant clearing of the throat caught my attention. Elizabeth lingered in the arched entryway eyeing me skeptically. "Mrs. Langmore would like to see you."

I stood and followed her. Her stiff body language suggested she wouldn't be receptive to anything I had to say. "What has Mrs. Langmore told you?"

Elizabeth slowed and turned around. She released a long

breath and lifted her eyebrows. "She's leaving the estate to my grandmother."

"Yeah," I said, wading in slowly, "Pretty incredible."

Elizabeth tipped her head. "Lin's going to have a hard time accepting it."

"Mrs. Langmore doesn't have any heirs," I stated matter-of-factly. I stepped to one side of the corridor to allow an elderly woman, who seemed especially spry strolling past with a walker that barely touched the burgundy carpet. I nodded. "Morning."

The resident's gaze lifted to mine, seemingly annoyed by my greeting. She rushed past. I was merely an obstacle. I caught Elizabeth's gaze and was rewarded with a crooked smile. "I think it's lunchtime," she said quietly.

"Must be. Hey, Elizabeth..." I stepped forward and reached up to touch her arm, then thought better of it. "This is a really good thing."

"I'm happy for Lin." Elizabeth acquiesced. "It's incredible really." She looked down briefly, as if gathering her thoughts. "I don't like how all this played out. But somehow you've convinced Mrs. Langmore to consider your plan." She narrowed her gaze almost imperceptibly. "It must be good because Mrs. Langmore hasn't lost a beat, even with age. She's not one to fall for your charm."

A smile pulled on the corner of my mouth. "So, you think I'm charming?"

Elizabeth rolled her eyes. "Let's see what has Mrs. Langmore so enamored."

elizabeth

"Ah, there you are." Mrs. Langmore planted her hand on the arm of the couch, ready to stand. "I thought maybe you two were making up out there."

"No need to get up," I said, sitting down next to her and ignoring the heat of embarrassment crawling up my cheeks. Perhaps living into her tenth decade had afforded the woman remarkable insight. Even I couldn't ignore Nicholas's magnetic pull.

Nicholas grabbed one of the kitchen chairs and dragged it to face the couch. Lin remained at the small kitchen table, seemingly lost in thought. It would probably take her a while to come to terms with her newly discovered good fortune.

"Sadly, I won't live forever," Mrs. Langmore said, jumping right in.

I reached over and took her hand. "Don't say that."

The older woman patted my hand. "I've lived a long life, and God willing, I still have some time, but I want to make plans so that things aren't left to chance. Nicholas, here, has a plan for the Langmore estate that I think we can all get behind."

The scraping of chair legs against the wood floor drew our

collective attention to my grandmother. "Any decisions are yours alone." Lin hoisted her chin, a determined set in her eyes.

"Yes, that's true," Mrs. Langmore said. "But I'm asking for your input because once I'm gone, the property will be your problem."

"My problem..." Lin shook her head, still dazed by her good fortune.

"Let's hear what Nicholas has to say," I said, my curiosity getting the better of me.

"Okay," Nicholas said, "my father has long wanted a boutique hotel on the lake, and there's no mistaking the Langmore home is on prime real estate."

"You're not going to allow them to tear your house down," I blurted out, another wave of anger hitting me.

Mrs. Langmore patted my hand. "Hear him out."

Nicholas flipped to another page. "I have a sketch...it's rough..." He locked gazes with me for a moment and I tried to deny the flutter in my belly. Thankfully, he dropped his gaze back to the paper. "I'd like to retain the integrity of the main house while refurbishing it to accommodate guests."

I stared at his drawing, my hopes deflating. Wasn't *I* going to update the house? Grow my social media influencer status? Be my own boss.

No, this is the solution. Nicholas and his team can handle a project of this magnitude. Then I can go back to Boston. Malissa told me about that job. It'll be perfect.

All the pieces are falling into place.

My heart thudded in my ears as Nicholas explained his plans of building a standalone structure set off to the side and connected by a covered walkway to the main house. The boutique hotel could host luncheons, meetings and weddings with a spectacular view of the lake.

"What do you think?" Mrs. Langmore asked, genuinely excited about the plan.

It's not a bad idea.

I waited for Lin to voice her opinion. The future of the Langmore estate was in her hands. "I...I..." Lin scrubbed a hand across her face. "Mrs. Langmore, if this is what you want."

"If the Morettis buy the land, you won't have to deal with the estate. It costs a fortune to maintain. You can pick up and go wherever you want," Mrs. Langmore said. "Perhaps you'd like to travel. You won't be anchored to Walleye Point."

A hurtful memory crowded me. My grandmother had grumbled about how becoming my guardian later in life had straddled her with a responsibility she hadn't been prepared for. Didn't want. Now, Lin could be free. Do whatever she wanted.

"I've always loved living on the lake." The vulnerability in poor Lin's expression softened my heart. She had done the best she could under the circumstances. She had lost a daughter. Had to raise a granddaughter. And now she was trying to process everything while her brain was healing from a stroke.

I wanted to reassure her that everything would be fine. More than fine, but I didn't trust I'd find the right words. Thankfully, Mrs. Langmore did. "Nothing has to be decided today. But you have options. One of which is doing nothing. But whether you like it or not, the Langmore estate or the proceeds from its sale are yours upon my death." The older woman touched the pendant at her neck. "Walleye Point is a small town. We might not ever get an offer like this again."

The wariness in Lin's eyes tugged at my heartstrings.

"Mrs. Langmore, your generosity is amazing." I gently squeezed her hand and stood. "I think Lin might need to rest. Can we discuss this again another day?"

"Of course," Mrs. Langmore said. "I'm sure Nicholas can meet with us at another time when we're ready to decide."

"Absolutely." Nicholas tapped the papers on the table to line up their edges. "You know where to reach me if you'd like to move forward." He smiled. *Oh boy, that smile.* "Have a good day."

After the door closed, Mrs. Langmore spoke quietly. "I didn't want to put you on the spot in front of Nicholas, either of you. What do you think?"

"I can't wrap my head around this." Lin dragged her hand through her thinning gray hair. "Nicholas seems like a nice enough young man, but I'll never forgive the Moretti family." Her agitation was visible in the firm set of her jaw.

"Nicholas assured me he would spearhead the project. He's a good man." Mrs. Langmore paused a beat before adding, "Don't cut off your nose to spite your face, Linda. This sounds like a wonderful opportunity. My home will get a second life."

Lin crossed her arms over her chest and shuddered. I stood. "Let's get you home." I smiled at the kindly woman and mouthed, "Thank you." I held out my hand and Lin stood, leaning heavily on me for support. "We'll talk and we'll be up to visit again soon."

Mrs. Langmore stood, and Lin reached for her hand and squeezed it. "You've been too good to me. I don't deserve it."

"You do. You deserve only good things." Then, turning to me, Mrs. Langmore added, "Maybe you can share your wonderful ideas with Nicholas. I bet he'd love to have a partner."

I tucked my chin, ready to disagree. However the knowing look in the older woman's eyes rendered me mute. Protesting would have seemed like too much.

29 /
elizabeth

When I pulled onto the Langmore property, I took it in with fresh eyes. All of this would be my grandmother's. *Unbelievable.*

I put the car in park and looked at Lin. "What do you think?" My grandmother had been quiet on the drive home.

"Mrs. Langmore will come to her senses," Lin said without much emotion. "The idea that she'd leave me this home is…" She shook her head in disbelief.

I climbed out of the car and jogged around to open her door. She needed some rest. "Let's get you inside."

Lin's eyes sparked with anger. "You're not going to treat me like an invalid, are you?"

I stuffed down the frustration bubbling at the back of my throat. The response was instinctual, automatic. A lifetime of conditioning. I released a slow breath. "Let's have lunch."

When we walked around to the front of the bungalow, Lin slowed. "What happened to all my stuff?" Her mouth narrowed.

I counted silently to ten. "I got rid of the garbage—"

"It wasn't garbage!" Lin shouted, her face growing red. "You had no right! I can't believe you'd do this to me!"

Always the victim. I did this for *you.*

"I always loved this porch," I said, gently leading Lin up the steps to the glider. "The furniture cleaned up well, didn't it?"

"It wasn't that bad," Lin muttered, clearly agitated.

"I only threw out the things that were ruined."

"There was no reason to throw out my belongings," Lin insisted, glaring at the lake, as if it had done her dirty. She refused to look at me. "I wanted to sort through everything myself."

"Anything of sentimental or real value is in the house." I prayed that would suffice. "We can go through the things together if you'd like." I chose my words carefully, afraid I'd set her off. Again.

"I don't need your help." Lin's mouth twitched.

I allowed the silence to settle between us. Lin would need time.

The sound of gravel crunching under tires made my heart race. Had Nicholas decided to stop by to pitch his plan again? No, he wouldn't do that. A car door slammed. I held my breath. Waiting. Half expecting Nicholas to appear around the side of the house, his cocksure grin ready to work on Lin's resolve. Instead, Cassie appeared in a matching set of scrubs in a flattering shade of purple with a Vera Bradley tote slung over her shoulder. "Hey there," she said.

"Hi." My pulse slowed. *Boy, for someone who claims I don't want anything to do with Nicholas, I sure am bummed he's not here.*

Cassie planted one foot on the bottom step. "Nice to see you home, Mrs. Graham. How are you doing?"

"Fine," Lin said, still seething.

Apparently sensing the tension, Cassie got right to it. "I've changed jobs recently and I'm doing some home nursing."

"Oh," I said, not hiding my surprise. Cassie seemed to have a great job in the hospital's ICU. "Needed a change?"

Something flickered across Cassie's expression and disappeared. "The beauty of nursing. Lots of different opportunities." She shifted her feet, seeming uncomfortable with the question. "If it's okay, Lin, I'll be your home nurse. I'll check your vitals once a day over the next few weeks. Make sure there aren't any trip hazards in your home. Things like that." She lifted an eyebrow and caught my gaze, perhaps acknowledging how different the place looked since the last time she had been here.

Lin huffed. "Will this ever end?"

I swallowed the instinct to apologize for my grandmother.

"Can we go inside? I'll need to check for those trip hazards," Cassie said. "Then I'll get out of your hair." The woman knew how to read a room.

Without waiting for Lin to agree, I unlocked the door. Lin got up on her own and followed them inside. Suspicion hardened her expression as she scanned the tidied kitchen and living room. If she could have identified something specific that was missing, she would have gone after me. As it was, Lin was probably too shocked at the drastic change to process anything.

"You've made a lot of progress. The place looks good," Cassie said, and as soon as she did, gooseflesh raced across my arms. I braced for Lin's reaction.

"You had people in my house when I wasn't here?" Lin snapped.

A knot tightened between my shoulder blades. My mind raced for a suitable answer, and I settled on the truth. "When you were in the hospital, you mentioned you had a dog. Cassie came by to check on him. She was doing you a favor."

"That's silly. I don't have a dog."

"You were a little confused," I said uneasily.

"Your brain is healing," Cassie explained. "I'm sure you're happy to be home."

Lin released a puff of breath from the corner of her mouth.

"Linda," Cassie said, in a cordial tone, "is it okay if I call you Linda? I'll be back tomorrow and we can go over your PT exercises."

Lin raised her hands in front of her as if to say *I've had enough* and shuffled across the worn carpet toward her bedroom.

"I'm sorry about that," I whispered. "This is the first time she's been in the house since we cleaned up."

"No worries. She's been through a lot." Cassie waved goodbye. "See you tomorrow."

After the nurse left, I checked on my grandmother who was watching TV in her bedroom. I wanted to say *Isn't it nice that you can watch TV from bed?* Clearing all the heaping piles of junk from every surface had made that possible. But I didn't want to press my luck.

"I have to run errands." I crossed the room and placed a phone on the nightstand. "Call me if you need anything."

"I'm fine." Lin tugged on the freshly washed crocheted blanket on her lap, the one that I had been looking for when I first came back to the bungalow. "I can't remember the last time I was able to lie in bed and watch TV."

I smiled. That might have been the closest thing to an expression of gratitude from Lin that I'd ever heard.

"I won't be gone long."

30 /
elizabeth

I climbed the steps to the business office above the Italian restaurant. *Moretti Realty and Construction* was etched on the frosted glass. I hadn't called ahead because I was afraid I would lose my nerve. I was about to knock when the door swung open.

Junior Moretti, Nicholas's father, stared down at me, but I refused to wilt. His bright eyes sparked recognition under his bushy gray eyebrows. "Hello, dear, how can I help you?"

"Um, hello." So much for catching Nicholas alone.

A moment later, Nicholas appeared behind his father, a warm smile on his handsome face. *Thank goodness.* "Hey there."

"Hi, um, do you have a minute?" I asked, feeling uncomfortable under the weight of the stares of the two Moretti men.

Nicholas stepped back. "Want to come inside?" Then to his dad, he said, "If you'll excuse us. We have some business to discuss."

"Turns out my youngest might have some chops in this business after all," the elder Moretti said before he turned and slowly navigated his way down the steep wooden steps hugging the back wall of the Italian restaurant.

Inwardly, I shook my head. The Morettis were used to getting their way. It almost made me want to rush down the steps, past Junior. A quick departure. A silent *Forget it. I don't need you. Either of you.* But that would be shortsighted. For Mrs. Langmore's—and Lin's—sake, I needed to explore all the options for the property. Perhaps I could present the proposal in a neutral fashion, without the negative history between our two families dating back to the night of the tragic accident.

I stepped into the office and took a seat, never growing tired of the amazing view of the harbor. Nicholas slipped behind the desk and leaned back, affecting a casual pose. "Hey there. I wasn't sure you'd be up to meeting with me. You've pretty much shut me out these past few weeks."

"And yet you popped up at Mrs. Langmore's," I said deadpan, struggling to hold on to a grudge. Was he really that bad of a guy? He was doing his job. Could I fault him for using all the angles—including me?

As if reading my mind, Nicholas said, "I wasn't trying to use you to get to Mrs. Langmore."

"Hmm..." I said, noncommittally. I had not been expecting him to be so forthright.

"The minute I saw you that first day, I was intrigued." He dragged his lower lip through his teeth and drew in a deep breath. "I wanted to get to know the woman with that fire in her eyes. The one who wanted to tell me and Dom to buzz off when we wandered onto Mrs. Langmore's property."

"I should have told you to get lost." Then maybe my heart and head wouldn't be twisted into a confused mess.

"I enjoyed spending time with you. I just wish we didn't have the complication of all this..." His hands hovered over the paperwork on his desk, papers that probably had to do with the Langmore Estate. "And I had no idea about our families' pasts." He shook his head, obviously preoccupied by the same concerns that had kept me away. But now, I was back, and he was confessing his feelings. Even still.

That's not why I'm here. My future is not in Walleye Point. Or with him.

"It's fine. We can move past that. I'd like to hear more about your plan for the Langmore property." *Yes, that's it. Keep it professional.* I wondered if my words sounded as breathy to him as they did to me.

"Of course." A slow smile spread across his face. His cheeks flushed with what I suspected was embarrassment. Had I done this to him? Made him all vulnerable and eager to explain his side of things? I fidgeted with my hands in my lap. "Mrs. Langmore is intrigued by your plans. Can you tell me more?"

"I'd love to." Nicholas pulled a manila folder from under a stack of papers and flipped it open. "First, I want you to understand that this would be my baby. My father and brothers would not be involved."

I furrowed my brow.

"My father assured me that if I closed this deal, this project would be mine." He tapped his fingers on the papers. "Junior Moretti can be ruthless and ultra-competitive, but most importantly, he's true to his word. Whether I do this or he does, he gets bragging rights that a Moretti broke ground on the new hotel and convention center in town."

I ran a finger across my lower lip. "Tell me more."

Nicholas went through the tentative plans, assuring me that the main house would remain standing with upgrades to allow for guest rooms. A new meeting center would be built to the back of the main house. Both with views of the lake. He paused and waited for me to meet his gaze. "Thoughts?"

"Interesting for sure. I'd want to see the formal plans." I leaned back in the chair, wondering if I could ever convince Lin to agree to sell since Mrs. Langmore valued my opinion.

"I haven't yet hired an architect." He closed the file. "I wanted to talk to one in particular."

A flush of goosebumps raced across my skin. *Oh no…*

"Would you consider signing on?" he asked.

"Well…" I stammered, "Mrs. Langmore hasn't sold you the property yet, and Lin would have to agree." That had been a stipulation of Mrs. Langmore's.

He tilted his head, and his brown eyes seemed to see into my soul. "Think about it."

I nodded, not trusting my voice. I pushed to my feet. "I should go. Lin's home alone."

Nicholas walked around the desk and stopped a respectable distance from me. "Was your grandmother pleased with the cleanup?"

I laughed, resisting the urge to step closer to him. "She nearly had my head. So…she's definitely on the mend."

Nicholas opened the door, and the fresh spring air cooled my flushed skin. "That's good, right?" He rested his shoulder on the frame of the door. "I'm here if you need anything."

"I appreciate it." I slipped past him onto the landing. The metallic clatter of silverware floated up from the open windows of the restaurant below. I rested a hip on the railing, not quite ready to go. "I understand why Mrs. Langmore is intrigued. It'll preserve her home and give new life to the property." I released a quick breath. "But it will be a tough, *tough* sell for my grandmother. She still harbors a lot of resentment towards your family for that car accident. Perhaps she believes deep down that your family hung my mom out to dry." I pushed off the railing. "So like I said, tough sell."

"I can't change the past." The intensity of his gaze made me look away. He took a step closer. "Where do *we* stand?"

I studied the lines in the wood grain of the railing. The sound of silverware clattering grew louder, then died down, as if someone had opened the back door of the restaurant. "I have a job interview in Boston."

Nicholas planted a hand on the railing by my hip, and heat shot up my side. "Is that your polite way of telling me we don't have a shot?" His tone was serious, but the glimmer in his eye suggested otherwise.

This jerk always gets his way, I reasoned, but it held no heat.

It was the same old argument, but its effect had lessened. He wasn't a jerk. Far from it.

I scooted along the railing, away from him. I needed to think. "It's my way of telling you we should probably keep this relationship professional. Nothing has changed." A hollow sensation expanded in the pit of my belly. My fifteen-year-old self couldn't imagine I'd turned down *the* Nicholas Moretti. The captain of the hockey team. The coolest kid in town.

Nicholas shifted and leaned against the railing next to me. "Okay, how do you want to do this?"

"Do this...?"

"Yeah, how do you want to present this to your grandmother? You wouldn't be here if you didn't think this offer was a once-in-a-lifetime opportunity. Without the burden of taking care of the Langmore estate, your grandmother would be free to travel and do whatever the heck she wants." Nicholas ran a hand across his jaw.

"And you'll be free to go about your life too."

Go about your life...

I steeled myself. If Mrs. Langmore was receptive to the idea, why shouldn't Lin? And Nicholas seemed to be trustworthy.

I've been fooled before. But what did it matter? In the end, if it was a good decision for Lin, why should it matter if Nicholas charmed his way into the deal?

I envisioned my grandmother sipping lemonade on the porch. I loved that glider and view as much as my granddaughter did. I found myself searching for the holes in his plan. "It's quite possible Lin would be happy living out her days sitting on the porch of the bungalow, drinking iced tea and playing Wordle on her iPad." No amount of money could replace that.

"May I talk to her again? I could bring some dinner over. From the restaurant. Maybe tomorrow?"

I tapped my fist gently on the railing. I'd never be able to walk away without letting this all play out. Decisions had to be made. I heaved a sigh. "Don't say I didn't warn you." I descended the first few steps and paused to glance over my shoulder. "My grandmother isn't a pushover like me." Because I was definitely a pushover if I was agreeing to another meeting between him and Lin. I rushed down the rest of the steps.

"I'll take that as a yes," he hollered after me.

"I like meatballs with my spaghetti," I shouted over my shoulder without turning around. "And tomorrow is fine."

nicholas

The next evening, I slipped into the restaurant's kitchen and found three to-go containers sitting under the warming light. "Is this my order?"

Gia popped out from behind the open stainless steel freezer door. "Yep, spaghetti and meatballs."

I tapped the top of the warm container with my open palm. "I appreciate it."

Gia crossed her arms and rested her hip on the counter, her cane hooked on its ledge. "Headed over to the Grahams?"

With a newfound understanding of how my aunt's past was linked to Elizabeth's mom's, I tried to sound casual. "Still trying to convince the powers-that-be to sell me the Langmore property." I snapped a plastic bag off the roll and packed the first dinner. "Seems Linda Graham might be the last holdout. She's not a fan of the Morettis."

"You mean she's not a fan of mine?" Gia picked up a tomato and sliced it with practiced precision. I gave her the space to talk, hoping she'd shed some light on the long-standing animosity between the two families. Hadn't they both suffered after the accident when they were teenagers? I had heard countless times about Gia's dashed Olympic dreams. Any other details of that night were overshadowed by Gia's plight. *Poor, poor Gia.*

My aunt paused, then began cutting another tomato. "It was a long time ago."

"Yeah," I said, deciding not to push. I never had. My aunt was the one who had to live with the decisions she had made as a teenager. I packed the other two dinners, brushed a kiss across my aunt's cheek. "Thanks. Wish me luck."

"Mrs. Graham wasn't always as hard as she is now." Gia seemed to be lost in a memory. "We'd go to their house after school and her mom would make us something to eat. Jenn would grumble about her mother, but it didn't seem any different from my relationship with my mom." Gia tossed the tomatoes into the salad then wiped her hands leaving a streak of reddish-orange on her white apron. "Losing her daughter had to be difficult." Gia averted her gaze. "I guess I'm just saying, if you take the time to chat with her, you might get to know the person who I knew way back then."

"I appreciate the insight." I considered the rough plans for the Langmore property, the ones I had sketched out. I might just need to make another change—one I had been thinking about—before I presented them to Linda Graham. I'd mark up the draft in the vehicle before I headed over.

I climbed out of my SUV at Linda's home and walked around to find Elizabeth and her grandmother sitting on the glider enjoying refreshments. As I climbed the porch steps, I hoisted the to-go bag and smiled. I had the plans safely tucked under my opposite arm in a folder. "Dinner is here."

Lin glanced over at her granddaughter. "You didn't tell me *he* was bringing our dinner."

An embarrassed smile curved the corners of Elizabeth's mouth. "He brought spaghetti and meatballs from the Italian restaurant." She glanced at me for quick confirmation. "What's not to like about that?"

Lin leaned back in the glider. "I'm not that hungry."

Elizabeth shifted on the cushion. "You said you were starving."

Lin pressed her lips together, refusing to budge on this.

Feeling like I was intruding, I set down the manila folder, then the to-go bag on top of it. "Why don't I leave the food here? You can eat whenever you're hungry." I took a step backward, not wanting to push this. "Want me to grab some plates and utensils from the kitchen before I go?"

"I'll come with you." Elizabeth picked up the bag and reached for the door handle.

I followed her inside. The tiny kitchen was dated but clean and smelled lemony. "Wow, this looks like a different place."

Elizabeth studied her fingers. "And I have the broken nails to show for my efforts."

"I can see Lin's not happy about my being here. I'll come back another time."

"You've gone through all the trouble," Elizabeth said, as if considering my offer.

"Ha, I placed an order and picked it up. I think I'll survive." I ran a hand across my jaw. "I'll leave the draft of the plan for the property. I made a few changes. Maybe you can share them with her." Hopefully, Elizabeth could read his rudimentary drawings. "It might sway Lin's decision."

"Oh?" Elizabeth's eyes sparkled.

"Yeah, I—"

"Hello, Mrs. Graham," a familiar voice reached us through the screen door. "I hope you don't mind me dropping by."

"It's my aunt," I mouthed. Keeping my voice low, I whispered, "Maybe I should run interference." Without waiting for an answer, I stepped back outside. "Hey there."

"I thought you guys might like dessert." Gia stood on the bottom step with an apple pie in her hands and an apprehensive look on her face.

Elizabeth slid outside, scooted around me, and accepted the pie. "That was very nice of you. Um…" Elizabeth glanced over at her grandmother, then back at Gia. "Would you like to join us for dinner?"

Gia shook her head. "I should get back to the restaurant." But her body language suggested she wasn't ready to leave. She probably came here for something other than dessert.

Lin remained on the glider with her arms tightly folded across her chest, determined to shut out the world.

Gia's shoulders relaxed, and she took a step toward Lin. "Mrs. Graham, I'd very much like to talk to you."

Lin glared up at my aunt.

"Please, maybe we all should talk," Elizabeth said, then to me, "Could you grab two chairs from the kitchen? I'll pour us some iced tea."

"Your dinner will get cold," Gia said, as if the dinner wasn't the only thing growing cold.

Elizabeth waved her hand in dismissal. "That's what an oven is for."

32 /
elizabeth

I filled four glasses. Gia took a long sip and stared at the lake. "Mrs. Graham, you always made the best iced tea." She was making pleasantries despite the charged energy in the air.

"I know, right?" I said, matching Gia's forced cheer. "I've tried to duplicate it, but I never could get it quite right." The ice in my glass clinked when I sat down next to Lin, who would have made a great statue.

Sitting ramrod straight in one of the stiff kitchen chairs Nicholas had brought out onto the porch, Gia rested the glass on her knee and smiled warmly. "I can't get over how much you look like your mom." I had heard that a lot, but it was always jarring. Soon, I'd be older than my mother ever got to be.

"I was sorry to hear about her passing," Gia said, growing somber, the comment directed to both of us. But only I answered.

"Thank you." A lump of emotion formed in my throat. It was true what they said about grief. Even after all this time…

I squeezed my grandmother's hand, wanting to give her both support and encouragement. "I enjoyed chatting with you the other day about my mom." I gently nudged Lin's arm. "Turns out I got my mom's brains."

Lin remained still next to me on the glider.

Gia gave us a watery smile. "Your mom was really smart. Probably the smartest kid in our class." She traced a finger down the condensation on the glass, apparently buying time for whatever had brought her here.

"Sounds like my mom." I smiled at the memory of Mom helping me with homework.

"I don't need to tell you this…" Gia's gaze slid over to Lin's, then back to mine. "Your mom was really good at graphic design. It was an elective in high school. She would have made a wonderful architect like you, but…"

"I came along." I finished for her. Mom had never once grumbled that I had messed up her plans. Unlike my grandmother, who never let me forget it. I pushed the thought aside. I was coming to realize Lin had done the best she could, undoubtedly unable to get past her own wounds. Her own grief.

"Yeah, you came along." Gia sipped her iced tea, seemingly to buy time. "I was with your mom when she took the home pregnancy test." Her focus was on Lin now. "She was terrified."

The legs of a kitchen chair scraped against the wood planks of the porch. Nicholas stood. "I'll give you privacy." He looked like he'd rather be anywhere else. I might have laughed if the emotions weren't so raw. Of course, the charming Nicholas Moretti would get squeamish over talk of this nature.

"You need to hear this, too." Gia chuckled softly. "Maybe not all of this, but I hope you don't mind." She leaned toward Lin, seeking her permission. Lin blinked slowly and nodded.

I grew lightheaded. This person in front of me was the closest I'd ever gotten to learning more about my deceased mother. Even more than my grandmother. Gia held the secrets that teenagers only shared with other teens. I swallowed hard, and I swore I felt a lump travel the length of my esophagus. "I can't imagine," I finally mustered.

"Oh, she was freaked," Gia continued. "But once the idea settled, she was determined to do right by you. She was going to go to college and raise you." Gia bit her trembling lower lip. "She was so strong. Nothing would get in her way."

Lin ran a hand under her nose and sucked in a breath.

"What do you know about my dad?" I asked, feeling an emptiness void of grief. I couldn't rightfully mourn a man I had never met. I hadn't meant to bring up my father in front of Lin, not yet, but having Gia here seemed like an opportunity that might not present itself again. Maybe Gia wouldn't be evasive this time.

"We probably shouldn't..." Lin's brittle voice trailed off.

"He was handsome. Popular." Gia plucked at an imaginary piece of lint on her pants. "We were all kids. Made dumb decisions." She paused briefly before adding, "Your mom and I had a falling out because he was dating both of us."

"Oh." The revelation was a sucker punch to my gut. I could feel Nicholas's eyes on me. Lin never mentioned this. *She probably didn't know.* And now, whatever wholesome images I had about my father went poof.

"I don't mean to hurt you, but there have been enough secrets. Too many." Gia ran an open palm across her mouth and shifted in her chair to stare over the lake, seemingly lost in a memory.

"The Morettis made sure Jennifer paid for that night," Lin spoke up for the first time. Venom dripped from her carefully chosen words. "She was forced to leave town because everywhere she went, people glared at her. Blamed her." She drew in a shaky breath. "Shamed her."

"I loved your mom." Gia held her gaze on the water. A soft breeze kicked up and ruffled her hair. "I hated that we let a guy get between us. But then the accident..."

There wasn't a day that I didn't think about my mom. She died when I was only twelve. It shaped my life, yet there was still so much I didn't know about her. Finally I found my voice. "I'm sure she loved you too." I reached over and gently touched Lin's knee. "She loved both of you."

Lin's eyes widened, then she seemed to fold into herself. "I was ashamed of how I behaved. I was so angry when my only daughter told me she was pregnant. I wanted so much more for her than I had." Her voice grew softer. "We would have mended fences if not for the accident. She couldn't go into town without everyone making comments. Calling her a drunk. A killer. It was just awful."

It felt like a million fire ants were crawling over my skin. I stood and crouched down in front of my grandmother, drawing her hands into mine. We searched each other's watery eyes. "I'm sorry I wasn't there for her. I've regretted it every day."

Gia turned, resting her chin on her shoulder. "My father made sure everyone knew your mother was to blame." It was as if Gia needed to finish the story she had come here to tell. "He made sure everyone felt sorry for me, poor Gia who missed her big opportunity in the Olympics." Her lower lip quivered.

I reached over with my free hand and touched Gia's knee. "I'm sorry. You lost a lot too."

Gia stared off into the middle distance. "I only have myself to blame." She cleared her throat. "I didn't know how to handle my anger toward Tate and your mom." At the mention of my dad's name, a ticking started to sound in my head. Gia's retelling continued, her voice growing softer, as if through a long tunnel. "We all had too much to drink that night, sure, but I was the one who hopped in the car and started to drive away. Jenn and Tate tried to stop me." She spoke in a steady voice void of emotion. "Tate stood in front of the car and refused to move. He offered to drive because I was so emotional. Turns out, he was drunker. Missed the curve and slammed into a tree. If it wasn't for me..."

"Tate?" My voice squeaked, my mind's eye flashing back to the news article.

Tate Chilton, 18, was killed in a one-vehicle accident on Shueles Road.

"My father was killed in that accident." Prickles raced across my scalp.

Gia nodded slowly, a tear tracking down her cheek. "Tate and I were thrown from the car. Your mother was in the back seat. She was the only one with a seat belt on." She sniffed. "He died instantly."

Nicholas stood and put a hand on his aunt's shoulder. "You were kids. You had an awful lapse in judgement. You can't keep beating yourself up."

Gia released a shaky breath. "It's worse than that. I was the one who provided the alcohol. I was the one who lied. Said Jenn bought it. I was afraid of my father. I didn't want to get in trouble."

"You lied," Lin said, as if trying the words out.

"There's nothing I can do to make this right, Mrs. Graham. Once the lie was out there, I couldn't go back," Gia said. "My father became my champion. For once, I could do no wrong and I didn't have to do anything but look pathetic. After dad died, my brothers took over for him, always muttering how the blasted Jennifer Graham ruined my Olympic chances. Killed that boy. It seemed easier to let someone else take the blame than to deal with my own culpability."

I released Gia's hand and exhaled sharply. A weight pressed on my chest. Now it made sense, the reason no one talked about my father. Had only made vague mentions of him being gone. Maybe it was meant to spare me the pain. I had no idea what to feel.

I turned and found Lin studying me. "I wanted to protect

you from such an awful thing." It was Lin's turn to take my hand. "I'm sorry."

"You did what you thought was best." The words fought against the lump of emotion in my throat. Lin had suffered so much, and I needed to extend her grace.

I worried that all this stress wasn't good for her recovery.

"I spent everything I had on legal fees," Lin said, her voice making her sound small. "Without Mrs. Langmore and this job, I would have become homeless."

"I should have come forward a long time ago," Gia said, "but I thought it would only bring up a lot of bad memories for everyone." Gia smoothed a hand down her thighs. "I'm done being a coward." Her gaze drifted from Lin to me and back. "I don't want you to hold what I did against my nephew. He's a good man." She cleared her throat. "If you want to sell this place, I can't think of anyone more honest and fair." She shrugged, then pushed to her feet. "I'm so, so sorry." She seemed to be choking on her emotions.

Nicholas touched his aunt's arm in a tentative gesture. My heart went out to this woman, despite everything. The pain seemed to roll off her in waves. I wanted to offer her absolution, but it wasn't mine to give.

"Let me drive you home." Nicholas held out his hand for his aunt. I nodded my understanding. Our visitors walked down the porch steps toward their cars.

Lin sat quietly, wringing her hands. She spoke so quietly at first that I couldn't make out the words. "I'm ashamed. I bear a lot of responsibility for chasing my sweet daughter away. I was more worried about what everyone else would think about her pregnancy. I should have let her know I'd stand by her side no matter what. Jennifer was the most important thing to me. She tried to tell me she didn't buy the alcohol, but I called her a liar. I blew up at her. Called her horrible names." She drew in a shaky breath. "My daughter needed me and I was too proud to help her. And I lost her forever."

I sat down next to Lin and pulled her close. "Mom loved you." I sniffed, fighting back tears. "She entrusted me to you in her will because she loved you so much. That was intentional. She knew she was dying." My voice broke. Mom understood that Lin had a rough upbringing. Jennifer, too, had messed up. My mother had found forgiveness in her heart.

"I should have done better." My grandmother lifted a shaky hand and tucked a strand of my hair behind my ear. It was such a gentle gesture, so unlike Lin. "I took all that anger out on you, too." She pressed her lips together. "I'm sorry." She looked around, as if realizing for the first time that the company had left. "Oh, I..."

Lin craned her head toward the driveway. "Go catch them. I want Gia to know that I forgive her. *Go. Go.* We've wasted enough time." Lin tapped a finger to her head and gave me a rueful smile. "That stroke must have messed me up." She laughed quietly, the tears in her eyes indicating her true emotions.

I pressed a kiss to her temple. "I'm glad you're home."

"Me too." Lin fluttered her fingers in a hurry-up gesture. "Go on now."

I ran around to the side of the house and found Nicholas and Gia talking quietly outside their vehicles.

"Hey." I pressed my hand to my chest, catching my breath. "Good...you're still here."

A soft smile played on Nicholas's lips. "What's up?"

I rolled up on my heels, suddenly very cognizant of the deeply personal nature of their conversation. I was just getting to know Nicholas, and I barely knew his aunt, and here they were airing out all their dirty laundry. "It would be a shame to let all that food go to waste," I said with forced humor.

"I have plenty at the restaurant," Gia said, discreetly wiping her cheek with the back of her hand. "Thank you all the same."

I took a step closer. "My grandmother would like to talk to you."

Gia flashed Nicholas a concerned smile, as if to say *I'm in for it now.*

"It's important." I shrugged, a gesture that contradicted the pleading nature of my request. "Besides, we can't possibly eat all that food alone. *Please.*" I added the last little bit as an enticement.

I followed Elizabeth as she led me towards the edge of the cliff while my aunt joined Elizabeth's grandmother on the porch.

"You and I can go down to the beach while they chat," Elizabeth suggested.

"You gonna risk these steps again?" I placed my hand on the small of her back as we started down the steps.

"I trust that providing better access to the lake is on those plans of yours?" Elizabeth glanced over her shoulder. The wind swept her hair across her face. I wanted to reach out and tuck it behind her ear but held back. Reviewing the details of the project had been put aside. It seemed that the families had to forgive each other in order to move forward.

I didn't want to shout over the wind, so I waited until we reached the bottom platform. She maneuvered to sit down, her feet dangling over the edge. A flirtatious smile played on her lips as she held up her hand. "Let's just sit here. I don't feel like doing acrobatics to get down to the beach." What she left unsaid was, "Like last time." The time not too long ago when our feelings began to grow.

I joined her, bumping shoulders as I got into position. I let silence settle around us. Fingers of purple and red streaked the sky with the setting sun. This location *was* perfect for a hotel, but I was sensitive enough to know now was not the time to bring it up.

Elizabeth was the first to speak. "My grandmother's stroke seems to have softened her heart. She's lived her life with a lot of hate and regret, but she's ready to let it go."

I took her hand in mine. I traced my thumb across the back of her hand. "I can't imagine the guilt my aunt carried because of that accident."

"They were kids."

"Scary how quickly things can change. A few bad decisions..."

"My grandmother doesn't want Gia to feel guilty." Elizabeth brushed a piece of hair away from her bottom lip. "That's why she wanted to talk to her."

I squeezed her hand. "Good."

I glanced down at her lips, then up into her eyes. "I didn't get close to you because I had hopes of purchasing this property. It just happened to be the way we met." My eyes pleaded for her to believe me. "I'll never forget seeing you that first time, looking up at Mrs. Langmore's house. My first thought was, 'Who is that?' But things quickly got complicated, didn't they?"

Elizabeth flattened her lips, then shifted her gaze beyond me to the water.

I traced a soft heart on the back of her hand. "The moment I saw you is etched into my brain. And no matter what your grandmother and Mrs. Langmore decide, I hope—"

"I have a job opportunity in Boston," Elizabeth blurted.

I lifted her hand to my lips. "How can I convince you to stay?"

elizabeth

A jolt of electricity shot up my arm from where Nicholas's warm lips had kissed the back of my hand. The expression in his eyes was so sincere it made my heart ache. *Can I stay? My dream life has always been in Boston.*

I smiled, trying to hide the rioting emotions swirling inside me. "Do you always get your way?" Could Nicholas hear how breathless I was?

Had I been using Boston as an excuse?

My escape. My home. I loved Boston. But I was growing to see another part of Walleye Point. *This* had once been home. My gaze flitted across the gorgeous lake. I had once found solace in this exact view.

"Do I always get my way?" Nicholas repeated my question, pulling my hand away from my face and running his thumb across it. Man, he made it hard to think straight. "My fate is in your hands." He slipped his hand around my elbow and drew me closer, shoulder to shoulder, as we sat on the platform, our feet dangling above the pebbly sand.

"You don't...*we* don't know each other that well," I whispered into the wind, as if that answered a question.

The warmth radiating off him made me want to lean into

him. Stay here forever. Could I? Stay here in Walleye Point? I had a hard time wrapping my head around the idea. From the moment I had moved to Walleye Point, I had wanted to leave.

I wasn't an impulsive person. I was a planner. A list maker.

"It's a shame if this ended because of…" Nicholas pressed his cheek to my head, seemingly struggling for the right word, "…proximity." His chest rose and fell with his obvious frustration. "You think I'd like Boston? I could get a job in sales or something."

I rolled my eyes and laughed. He wasn't being serious. *Is he?* He was a Moretti. His life, his business was woven into the fabric of Walleye Point. *Nicholas Moretti* would never leave this town.

When the silence dragged a beat too long, I asked, "You're not serious."

"Why not?" He shifted on the platform to look into my eyes. He took both of my hands in his. "Maybe it's time for a change. Time to get out from under the shadow of my father. The Moretti name."

I had a hard time wrapping my head around the notion that this man—this handsome, strong, confident man—doubted his own abilities. "Do I need to remind you of all the things you've accomplished? Your dad wasn't on the ice with you when you won States in high school."

Nicholas rocked back and released one hand. Closing it into a fist, he pressed it into his gut as if he had been stabbed. "Yikes, did I peak in high school?"

The exaggerated look of anguish on Nicholas's face made me laugh. "You know what I meant. There are so many accomplishments you could rattle off—things that I don't know yet—that could only have been accomplished because you're *you*. Not your dad or your brothers." I twisted to look up the cliff; only the highest peak of Lin's bungalow was visible from this angle. "You're on the verge of buying this land, creating a new life for this property. Mrs. Langmore—and oh, don't get me started on my grandmother—are only considering your proposal because it's *your* proposal. Because of what you've brought to the table."

Nicholas gently tugged my hand, drawing me closer. I had to plant a hand on his solid chest to avoid falling into him. He pressed his cool lips to mine, lingering for a long moment before pulling away. A slow smile curved his lips. "You really know how to prop a guy up."

I exhaled and shook my head. "Did you just play me?" Pretend he'd give everything up for me? I dragged the back of my knuckles across his whiskered jaw. *Man, he does things to me.* I softly cleared my throat and forced a playful smile, one that didn't reveal the depth of my emotions. "You wanted me to feel sorry for you so I'd..." I pulled my hand away from his grasp and used air quotes, "Prop a guy up."

"I'd never do that." He tapped my nose and followed it with a soft kiss.

A brisk wind swept my hair up and away from my neck. I shuddered, but it was only partially due to the cool breeze. This man had such an effect on me.

"Come on." Nicholas got to his feet and extended a hand. "We should probably head up. It's getting cold."

We held hands as we navigated the rickety steps up the side of the cliff. When we reached the top, I glanced backward. "First thing on your list is these stairs."

Nicholas made an imaginary checkmark in the air. "Done."

I leaned into him and whispered. "Look at that." Gia and Lin were laughing and chatting on the glider. Lin's features appeared softer and her eyes brighter. Forgiveness seemed to lighten her.

I tugged Nicholas by the hand toward the porch. "The beach was breezy," I said, as if apologizing for interrupting them.

Gia slid to the edge of the cushion, then stood. She seemed to take them in, from head to toe. Feeling self-conscious, I dropped his hand.

"It is getting late." Gia turned to Lin. "Thanks for…this."

Lin folded her hands on her lap. "It was good for both of us. I hope you won't be a stranger."

Nicholas climbed the two steps to the porch to say good-night to my grandmother. Meanwhile Gia approached me. "Nicholas is a good man. I hope you stick around long enough to find out."

"I um…" I shrugged, acting like I didn't know what Gia meant, but realized Nicholas and I weren't fooling anyone.

Gia tilted her chin toward the porch. "Your grandmother seems pretty excited about the possibilities for this property," she added. "Especially the plans for her bungalow."

"Oh?"

"My nephew left a folder on the porch. We took a peek."

My fingers itched to get a hold of those plans.

"Don't believe anything she says." Nicholas jogged toward us with a big smile on his face and a manila folder tucked under his arm.

Gia touched my arm, then let it drop. She tilted her head toward the car. "I'm going to head out." She flicked her hand in a casual wave. "Hope to see you around."

"Good night," I called out after her.

The screen door clacked in its frame as my grandmother disappeared inside. I turned back to Nicholas and found him studying my face.

"What plans do you have for Lin's place?" I reached for the folder tucked under his arm, my curiosity besting me.

Nicholas playfully batted my hand away. "Nope."

"Gia and Lin said they looked at the plans." I inwardly cringed at my whiny tone. I squared my shoulders. "I would love to have a look."

A slow smile curved his handsome mouth. "I sketched out

the property line to allow Lin to keep her bungalow. We'll make the necessary updates to her home and add landscaping for privacy. There's no reason she would have to move. If that's what she wants."

"Oh, wow, I'd like to see that," I said, reminding myself it wasn't good form to have grabby hands.

He reached up and cupped my cheek. He placed a long, lingering kiss on my lips. When he pulled away, he spoke in a husky breath, "It's late. Let's meet tomorrow?"

"What time?"

"We'll meet here when it's daylight. I'll walk you through the plans." His hand traveled down my arm, leaving a trail of tingles in its wake. "So? Tomorrow?"

"Tomorrow." I crossed my arms and watched him leave. *Oh my, oh my…*

35 /
elizabeth

I took my coffee and laptop out onto the porch. It was a gorgeous spring day. I turned the camera around to show Malissa on the other end of the call. "I can't get enough of this."

Malissa leaned back in her office chair, slowly shaking her head. "Are you telling me you're not coming back?" My college roommate glanced over her shoulder at the views outside her Boston high rise. "And give up all this?"

Flames of panic and indecision licked the sides of my neck. "I didn't say that."

Malissa planted her elbow on the desk and rested her chin on the heel of her hand. "But you're not sure."

"I'm not," I said. "That's why I called. I don't want to burn any bridges, but I also don't want to waste your firm's time with an interview. I plan to stay in Walleye. For a little longer anyway." An image of Nicholas's handsome face came to mind. "I'd like to help Lin get settled, and this thing I'm starting on social media is taking off." I shrugged. "I think I need to give it more time. I might be able to make a go at this. It'd be great to work for myself."

"I've been lurking on your socials. You have a knack." Malissa smiled. "You've always had great ideas. That's why I liked teaming up with you when we had team projects in college."

"We made a great pair, didn't we?" Unexpected tears burned the back of my eyes. When I left Boston, I had figured it would only be temporary.

"Mmmhmm…we did." Malissa leaned toward the screen. "Does Nicholas have anything to do with this decision?"

I pressed my lips together, as if to say, *I'm not telling.*

"I can't wait to meet him. Has he ever been to Boston?"

Funny, he had mentioned following me to Boston last night, but he had only been kidding, right? His life was here.

"I'm not sure." I tucked a strand of hair behind my ear as a soft breeze blew in off the lake.

"Well, then you'll have to bring him up this summer to see the Aquarium and go on a Duck Tour."

"I've never been on a Boston Duck Tour," I said, dreading the idea of driving what seemed to be a perfectly good bus into the harbor.

"You're such a chicken." Malissa laughed, then suddenly grew somber. "I'm glad my smart college roommate is finally following her heart."

I opened my mouth to protest—it was a reflex—when Malissa lifted her hand, her index finger in clear view of the camera. "Oh, I have to go." The screen suddenly went blank. I closed the laptop and leaned back and smiled, feeling a level of contentedness I hadn't felt in…forever.

I set the laptop aside and stared over the lake.

"You don't have to stay to babysit me. I'll be fine." Lin appeared on the inside of the screen door. Apparently, she had been eavesdropping on the call. I anticipated a guilt trip that never came. "But if you decide to stay, it'll be wonderful to have you around."

I stood and turned toward the door, not trusting my voice. Lin lifted a hand and gave me a dismissive wave. "Now don't get all mushy on me." She shook her head. "I'm going to take a shower. Then I have some things to sort through." She shuffled away, her slippers making a nostalgic flapping sound against the kitchen floor.

I strolled to the porch's edge and braced my hands on the railing. My tough, unsentimental grandmother had shown me some heart. People *could* change. I was willing to meet her wherever she wanted.

"Hey there."

I snapped my head around to find Nicholas standing on the grass on the side of the porch. I pressed a hand to my racing heart. "Oh, you scared me. I didn't hear your car."

"I parked in front of the main house."

I glanced at my smartwatch. "Sorry, I didn't realize it had gotten so late." We had agreed to walk through Mrs. Langmore's home and discuss the plans, followed by lunch and more discussion. I ran a hand over my hair. I had hoped to—I wasn't sure what? Put on a little lipstick? Fix my hair?—before he got here.

"You need a few minutes?"

"Um, no." Lin was in their only bathroom anyway. "Let me get the keys for Mrs. Langmore's house." I rushed inside and set my laptop on the kitchen table. I took a minute to glance around. Lin's place needed updates, but it was tidy and clean, a stark contrast from when I first arrived several weeks ago. I snagged the keys off a hook and pushed through the screen door.

Nicholas held out his hand, inviting me to walk ahead of him. I paused on the pathway leading to the front door of the Victorian. The warm weather brought with it more weeds pushing through the cracks. I glanced up, up, up, at the widow's walk. The structure that had sparked an interest in architecture for a lost young girl.

Nicholas slowed and placed his hand on my back. "A penny for your thoughts?" He reached into his pocket and pulled out a paperclip and a piece of lint. He shrugged. "Turns out I don't carry cash."

I laughed. "Just as well. My ideas are worth far more than that."

He narrowed his gaze, confusion and hope sparked in his eyes.

"Like, if I decide to come onboard as the architect on this project...I'm not cheap." I scraped my teeth across my bottom lip, a gesture that seemed to mesmerize the man standing in front of me.

Nicholas reached out and took my hands in his. "You're thinking about staying? Working on this project."

A warmth expanded in my chest. "I want to preserve Mrs. Langmore's home. Give it a second life. And..." I snagged my device out of my back pocket, "...and work on this passion project." I flashed him one of my social media posts.

"I think you should. You've really got an eye."

"You've been following me?"

"Is that creepy?" Humor flashed in his eyes.

I shrugged, secretly pleased he had taken an interest. "That's why I post. To get followers."

He slid the phone from my fingers. "Maybe we could take a selfie now—with both of us—for your socials." He flashed a grin. "I bet you'll get a lot of likes."

I rolled my eyes and snagged the phone back from him. "I post images of things of architectural interest."

Nicholas spun me around, hugged me to his chest, and pressed his cheek to mine. "Come on. Snap the photo. Frame it so the house is in the background. It'll be the 'before' to document the transition to Walleye Point's new boutique hotel."

Relishing the feel of Nicholas's solid chest and his freshly shaven cheek, I swiped my hand across the screen and lifted the phone. As my finger was about to snap the photo, he planted a warm kiss on my neck.

"Oops, my bad," he said. "Take another." This time we both smiled into the camera. The home that had been in the Langmore family for over a hundred years rose over our heads, waiting to be transformed for the next generation to enjoy.

"Let me see." Nicholas studied the image over my shoulder. "Oh, that's a keeper."

I smiled, unsure if I wanted to post my personal life all over my professional social media accounts. *That's a problem for another day.*

"Let's see your plans for this place." I slipped out of his grasp and raced up the steps. I unlocked the door while Nicholas grabbed files from the front seat of his vehicle. I held the door open with my back and took a peek at the first photo on my phone, the one of Nicholas kissing my neck.

A million butterflies fluttered in my belly. I held the device against my chest as Nicholas jogged into the house. "Wow, this is really nice." He was referring to the gorgeous old home. I couldn't help but take another peek at the photo of us and agree.

Yes, yes, it is. A keeper, for sure.

I clicked on my favorite social media site and uploaded the photo. My thumbs quickly tapped out #VictorianRenovation #LakeErieLiving #ArchitectureLovers #ThisOldHouse #HistoricHomes. I glanced around the entryway of Mrs. Langmore's home. Nicholas spread out the plans on a long side table. A rush of excitement for the future washed over me. Turning my attention back to the photo, I added #BuildingOurFuture #CoupleGoals #Heartfilled #NewBeginnings.

I reread the post and before I hit "Send," I added one more: #HappilyEverAfter.

Dear Reader,

Thank you for reading *A FINE MESS*. Cassie's story is up next. Grab *CACHE ME IF YOU CAN*, the next closed-door romance in the Walleye Point Series of small-town romance.
Happy Reading,
Alison

also by alison stone

Walleye Point: Small-Town Sweet Romance

A Fine Mess: Book 1

Cache Me If You Can: Book 2

Hunters Ridge: Amish Romantic Suspense

Plain Obsession: Book 1

Plain Missing: Book 2

Plain Escape: Book 3

Plain Revenge: Book 4

Plain Survival: Book 5

Plain Inferno: Book 6

Plain Trouble: Book 7

Plain Secrets: Book 8

Hunters Ridge Series: Amish Romantic Suspense (The Complete 8-Book Boxed Set)

A Jayne Murphy Dance Academy Cozy Mystery

Pointe & Shoot

Final Curtain

Corpse de Ballet

The Complete Jayne Murphy Mystery Series (Includes all 3 Books)

———

For a complete list of books visit

Alison Stone's Amazon Author Page

———

about the author

Alison Stone is a ***Publishers Weekly bestselling author*** who writes sweet romance, cozy mysteries, and inspirational romantic suspense, some of which contain bonnets and buggies.

Alison often refers to herself as the "accidental Amish author." She decided to try her hand at the genre after an editor put a call out for more Amish romantic suspense. Intrigued—and who doesn't love the movie *Witness* with Harrison Ford?—Alison dug into research, including visits to the Amish communities in Western New York where she lives. This sparked numerous story ideas, the first leading to her debut novel with Harlequin Love Inspired Suspense. Four subsequent Love Inspired Suspense titles went on to earn ***RT magazine's TOP PICK!*** designation, their highest ranking.

When Alison's not plotting ways to bring mayhem to Amish communities, she's writing romantic suspense with a more modern setting, sweet romances, and cozy mysteries. In order to meet her deadlines, she has to block the internet and hide her smartphone.

Married and the mother of four (almost) grown kids, Alison lives in the suburbs of Buffalo where the summers are gorgeous and the winters are perfect for curling up with a book—or writing one.

Connect with Alison Stone online:
www.AlisonStone.com
Alison@AlisonStone.com

www.ingramcontent.com/pod-product-compliance
Lightning Source LLC
Chambersburg PA
CBHW031558310726
48974CB00003B/724